Twelve Bright Trumpets

"Reprinted in the Interest of Children"™
By American Home-School Publishing

American Home-School Publishing
5310 Affinity Court
Centreville, VA 20120-4145
(800) 684-2121

The poem "The Scribe" from THE ROMANESQUE
LYRIC: STUDIES IN ITS BACKGROUND AND DE-
VELOPMENT FROM PETRONIUS TO THE CAM-
BRIDGE SONGS, 50-1050 by Philip Schuyler Allen.
Copyright (c) 1928 by the University of North Carolina
Press, is used by permission of the publisher.

First AHSP Printing, May, 2004
ISBN: 0-9667067-5-7

Twelve Bright Trumpets

By Margaret Leighton

Cover Illustration by Alexander Elkorek

This book is
dedicated to my mother.

- Margaret Leighton

Foreword

There is something that I should like you boys and girls who are my readers to understand before you begin this book. These are stories, not actual history. But although the youngsters who are the chief characters are imaginary and their adventures as individuals are fiction, the settings, the customs and ideas of the people pictured here are as true to the period as long and careful study could make them. The large events that are the backgrounds for the stories are now a part of our history. Moreover, whenever an historical character does appear, like Vortigern or Charlemagne or Alfred, he is doing only what records tell us that he actually did do.

Of course these stories can show only brief moments in the long period of years that we know as the Middle Ages. I think that it might help you to understand the progress of history if you will think of it as a stream or river. It changes constantly; it is fed from many sources; there are rapids and eddies, great destructive floods and long, calm stretches. It is always moving, but always it is the same river from its beginning to its end. Strange and remote though these days may seem, every boy or girl who reads this book has a different world to live in now from what he would have had if, for instance, the barbarian chiefs that Gaius saw had not come to live in Kent, if thousands like Denis had not gone on the Great Journey, if Geoffrey's earl had not stood fast with the other barons at Runnymede, if the "sorcery" that Karl saw brewing in the dark workshop had not been, in truth, a noble magic.

Contents

ROMAN STANDARD-BEARER.

T*he End and the Beginning*

A LONG, LONG TIME AGO people called Celts[1] lived in the country that we now call England, or Britain. Compared to the people who lived in Rome and in parts of Greece and Egypt at that time, the Celts were uncivilized. Their ways of living were much like those of the American Indians when Columbus discovered America.

About 55 B.C. (this means fifty-five years before Jesus was born) Julius Caesar, a great Roman general, led an army to the island of Britain. He and his soldiers conquered some of the Celts who lived in the southern part of the island. These Celts, he said, were dressed in animal skins. They had blue eyes, long, light hair, and they stained their bodies

1. Pronounced either *Selts* or *Kelts*.

1

with dark blue dye. Their houses were made of poles and twigs and had no windows.

Because Caesar and his soldiers did not stay in Britain, the Celts did not remain conquered very long. About a hundred years later, another Roman general was sent to bring them once more under Roman rule. The general's name was Agricola. He and his soldiers conquered the people as far north as the country we now call Scotland. There he built a large wall to keep out the savage tribes of the northern part of Britain.

More than three hundred years passed and Rome had many rulers. Many people from Rome came to live in Britain. During all that time the Celts stayed under Roman rule. They became civilized and learned to build houses like those in Rome. They dressed and talked like Romans. When Hadrian, one of the great Roman Emperors, came to Britain in the year 121 he found a country filled with roads and cities.

Unfortunately the people in the civilized parts of Britain were constantly being attacked by savage and warlike people of the North. These people were called Picts and Scots. The wall that Agricola built did not keep all of them out, so Hadrian built another wall, south of that built by Agricola. Into this wall were built watch towers and every four miles a fort was set up.

The people of southern Britain were not the only ones who were being attacked by enemies. For many years the great city of Rome itself was in danger of being captured by warlike peoples from northern and eastern Europe. At last it became necessary for the

Roman soldiers in Britain to return to Rome to defend that city against attack.

The story you are about to read tells of a boy who lived in Britain during the time that Rome was calling back its soldiers, more than four hundred years after Julius Caesar invaded Britain. The boy's father was one of the soldiers who fought, at Hadrian's wall, to protect the British people against the fighting tribes of the north.

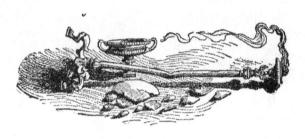

The cart rattled and jounced over the bumpy road. Gaius, wakened by an especially heavy bump, sat up on the pile of straw in the bottom of the cart and tried to look about him in the darkness. Where was he? Why wasn't he on the soft, cushioned couch in his own room? *Then* he remembered!

It had been so sudden! Gaius had been sleeping, just as usual, and then all at once the night had been full of noise and confusion. "What is it?" he had asked his mother, who was shaking him frantically.

"Get up and dress, my son!" his mother said. Gaius saw that her hand was trembling so much that the light of the bronze lamp she held flickered on the polished marble of the floor. "Waste no time! Word

3

has come that the Northern pirates are upon us!"

Gaius did not need further warning. Every child along the coast of Roman Britain had heard frightening tales of the roving shiploads of fierce, fair-bearded warriors who swooped in suddenly from the sea, setting fire to houses and killing men, women, and children.

Gaius had tumbled out of bed and dressed himself as fast as he could. He put on his short, belted tunic and his laced sandals. His mother caught up a woolen cloak and wrapped it about his shoulders. Then she hurried him out into the long porch upon which all of the sleeping rooms opened. Down the marble steps they ran together, while the torches in their tall holders flared on either side.

The grass and flowers in the open courtyard were being heedlessly trampled down by terror-stricken household slaves who ran in and out through the gateway in the high brick wall as they loaded carts with everything of value that was movable.

"Where are we going?" asked Gaius, as old Bleddoe, the freedman who was overseer and manager of their whole farm, lifted him into one of the carts."

"To the town. Its walls will keep the pirates out. I have already sent a man there on our swiftest horse with a message to the soldiers who are guarding the town," answered Bleddoe as he climbed into the seat and picked up the reins. Gaius's mother seated herself on the straw beside Gaius, where a group of slave women and children were already crouched, trembling and crying with fear.

"Everyone is out of the house—go forward, Bleddoe!" cried Gaius's mother. Bleddoe snapped the lash of his long whip with a loud crack, and the sturdy, shaggy little horse plunged forward.

They passed through the gate in the outer wall. This palisade of pointed timbers enclosed the whole group of farm buildings as well as the house. As the cart left the gate, Gaius saw the sky just over the hill to the north turn suddenly red. "Look!" he said, and his mother caught her breath.

"They have set fire to the village!" she told him. "But at least the people there were warned in time— they, too, have fled inland to the town."

Ahead of them in the darkness Gaius could hear other carts. The dust raised by their wheels was heavy and pale in the faint moonlight.

Cattle, sheep, and pigs were being driven along by their herdsmen. They formed a steadily moving river on both sides of the road. "Will the pirates burn our house, too?" asked Gaius as he looked back over his shoulder at the dark roofs of what had been his home for all of his ten years.

"I'm afraid they will. But we must not forget that we and all our faithful servants are safe. We have that much to thank Heaven for!" said his mother, as she watched the flames that rose and fell upon the horizon. "Your father sent me word months ago that we should leave the country and go into the town," she said sadly. "But I loved our home, our villa there on the white cliffs above the sea. I could not believe that these Northmen had grown so bold! Do they fear nothing—not even the power of mighty Rome!"

Gaius's father was far from home. He was a soldier, an officer in one of the legions, or armies, which guarded the peaceful British people from the tribes of uncivilized savage enemies all around them. Ever since Rome had conquered and colonized the island of Britain, three hundred years before, the worst of those enemies had been the wild Northern peoples known as the Picts and the Scots. To keep them out, a strong wall had been built across miles of country, from one sea to another. Soldiers kept watch day and night beside this wall. There, far in the North, Gaius's father had been stationed for almost a year.

But now new enemies were appearing more and more often along the unguarded seacoast. Why these Northmen had begun to leave their homes in the swamps and forests across the stormy sea, no one knew. For many years the ocean had been a protection to Britain, but now it did not prevent these bold warriors from attacking. It seemed almost to be an open highway for their long, beak-prowed ships!

Gaius lay in the straw at the bottom of the cart and looked up at the stars so high above him. He saw that the sky was now beginning to turn bright in the east. A sound, different from the creak and clatter of the carts or the slowly plodding hoofs of the tired horses, came to his ears. Gaius lifted his head. "What is that?" he asked.

Instantly his mother sat straight beside him. Her face was white and strained in the faint light of dawn. "It can't be the raiders—the noise comes from ahead of us," she said with relief. "It's soldiers! Our soldiers! At last we are safe!"

Sure enough, over the hill, riding swiftly down to meet them came a troop of soldiers on horseback. The bronze and polished brass of their armor and the spear-points above them glittered in the first long rays of the rising sun. The drivers of the carts pulled aside to clear the roadway, and the cavalry thundered past, leaving a long trail of dust behind them.

"They'll soon drive those pirates back into the sea!" cried Gaius joyfully.

Old Bleddoe shook his head. "The Northmen are fearless and mighty fighters, young master," he said. "They strike swiftly, take what they want, and destroy the rest. Unless they are far outnumbered, they never are conquered. But a troop of armed cavalry, experienced soldiers of the legion—perhaps that will be another story."

Now, from a hilltop, Gaius and his mother looked across the valley, cut by the bright curve of a river, to the town that was to give them safety. They could see the yellow brick buildings in the town as well as the high wall of rough stone and the deep ditch that encircled it. Gaius recognized the great church, or basilica, that stood almost in the center of the town. There he had gone to worship whenever he ad visited the city, for he and all his family were Christians. On a little hill above the open market place he saw the gleam of white pillars. There stood the temple where those of the townspeople who still believed in the old Roman gods went to make their offerings.

Finally they reached the wall of the town. Here a guard in a helmet of shining bronze looked down from a tower upon the little line of carts. Almost at once the huge wooden gate swung open to let them in, for the guard had recognized Gaius and his mother. The captain of the soldiers who guarded the wall came to meet them. Gaius greeted the man, for he was a friend of his own father.

"As soon as your messenger brought news of your danger I sent soldiers," the captain said to Gaius's mother. "I hope that they have saved your villa from destruction. Did you know that your husband Flavius is expected in the city today? He has been called here from his duty of guarding the Northern wall. There is soon to be a meeting of the Great Council of Britain. Vortigern, Prince of Kent, is here. He is camped just beyond the town. Ambrosius is here and all the leaders of Britain. The city is crowded with their followers, but I think you can find room somewhere to stay until you know whether your home has been saved."

"First of all, we must go to the church to give thanks for our escape," said Gaius's mother. "I think that the guest-house there will receive us." Just then a messenger spoke to the captain who excused himself and hurried away.

As they entered the porch of the church, Father Paul, the white-bearded priest, greeted them with surprise and pleasure, but his face was sorrowful when he heard the reason for their coming. "It is the same all over our poor land!" he said. "Everywhere the pitiless heathen make war upon us! What is to become of our people? Are we to live again like hunted animals of the forest, after all that Rome first, and then our Christian Church, has taught us of civilized living?"

Close by the high-walled church stood a monastery in which there was a guest-house for travelers. Here food was set before Gaius, his mother, and their servants. Fruit and fresh oat-cakes, milk, honey, and cheese were laid out on the long wooden tables. Gaius had not realized until then how hungry he was! He ate every crumb of his share. Then, with old Bleddoe, he went across the town to the great public baths. The warm pool, the steam room, the rubbing and drying rooms soon took the tired ache from his body. He splashed vigorously in the cool, fresh-water pool that was the last stage of his bath.

Gaius was telling the story of his night's adventures to a group of round-eyed town boys when Bleddoe entered the baths and excitedly called his name in a cracked old voice. "The Master has arrived—your father, Flavius himself!" Gaius dressed himself as quickly as he could.

How splendid Flavius looked in his gleaming armor and the tall helmet with its waving plumes! He pressed the boy close in his arms. His stern training in the Roman army had taught him not to show his feelings, but Gaius knew that his father was thinking how close the danger had come to his son last night!

"The Great Council is gathering, and I must go there at once," said Flavius. "If you wish to come with me, and will stand quietly behind my chair, you may hear the words that decide the fate of Britain!"

The council hall of the city was a large building which faced the public square. Outside, it was of the same yellowish brick as the rest of the buildings, but the inside was richly decorated. Marble paved the floor, and two rows of marble pillars ran the length of the wide room. Among the grave-faced men who sat upon the benches, Gaius recognized such leaders as the Count of Britain, the Roman officer who was in command of all the armies; the Count of the Saxon Shore, whose duty it was to guard the coasts of Britain; the noble Ambrosius, the most famous of all the Roman-Britains; and one other who, from his proud face and handsome clothes, Gaius knew must be Vortigern himself, Prince of Kent, whose ancestors had been kings in Britain before the Romans came.

Gaius was still staring about the hall when the leader of the Council rose to speak. Much of what he said was hard for Gaius to understand, but he could see that the faces of all the men grew more and more serious. All over Britain, it seemed, there was war and trouble.

"You will remember that we sent letters to Rome, begging for more soldiers to help us against these many enemies of ours," he said. "Rome has replied at last. And the reply is the reason for my calling together this Council. Rome itself will soon be attacked! Thousands of other savage warriors from the North have spread over all of Gaul and Italy. Now they are at the very gates of Rome! Not only from the forests of the North, but from the plains of the East these enemies have come! Rome cannot send us help in our need.

Indeed, orders have reached us to send back the last of the Roman legions. They must return to defend the city of Rome!"

Such a silence followed these words that Gaius could almost hear the pounding of his own heart! Withdraw the legions! Leave Britain defenseless, unprotected! Each man turned slowly and looked at his neighbor, as though he could not believe what he had heard.

At last one man rose to his feet. It was Ambrosius. As Gaius watched, he wondered how Ambrosius could look so calm and unafraid after what the leader of the Council had told the men. "This is indeed a blow to our hopes!" he said. "But at least the orders are to withdraw only the *Roman* legions. Those that are made up of soldiers who are British-born are to remain. We have them as a protection now and can use them as a beginning of a new army. Among them are such officers as Flavius here. Surely they can train and arm more of our own citizens to defend the borders of Britain! Before the Romans came, Britons fought their own battles!"

Gaius was thrilled by the brave words and the praise of his own father, but the other members of the Council seemed timid and doubtful. "Training of soldiers takes time," said one man.

"Our people have lived in security too long—they have forgotten how to fight," said a second man.

And a third added, with fear in his voice, "When they learn that the Roman legions have gone, the Picts and the Scots will come over the wall and down upon us with a fury never known before. And if we have the coast to guard as well..."

Again there was silence. Gaius looked anxiously about the circle. Surely among all these great, wise men, there would be found a plan to save the country!

Then he saw Vortigern, Prince of Kent, stand up and face the Council. Vortigern pushed the cloak back from his shoulders, and Gaius could see the richly jeweled embroidery on his tunic and the glitter of a golden chain about his neck. "All the tribes that live across the northern sea are not our enemies," said Vortigern. "Some of the Northmen have been helped by Rome in times past. Here in my camp are two chieftains, leaders of the Angles and the Saxons. Their warriors are many and strong. They feel only friendship and good will for us. They have sworn to me that they will stand by our side and defend Britain against Pict, Scot, or other Northmen, if, in return, we will let them live as equals among us. In return for their help, I, for one, am willing to give them homes in Kent—where, as you know, there is the best and richest soil in Britain. Let me send for them to come here now and tell you themselves about their plan."

The effect of the Prince's words upon the Council was almost like magic. All around the room the faces of the men were lighted with a new hope. Some, it is true, could not agree with the Prince's plan. Would heathens and savages, such as these chieftains were, keep their promises? One man cried aloud in fear that it was only a trick to get their warriors into Britain. But at last a messenger was sent to the camp of Vortigern. In a short time the Angle and Saxon chiefs stood in the pillared hall.

Never had Gaius seen men so tall! Their hair and the long beards that hung down upon their chests were as yellow as ripe corn. Their dress was strange to Gaius's eyes for they wore the fur of wild beasts and roughly made armor. Huge, two-handed swords hung by their sides. On the helmet of one were set sharp, spreading horns—those of a great wild ox. On that of the other, metal wings were fastened. As Gaius stared, the two chiefs glanced about the crowded hall, and one of them caught the boy's wide-eyed gaze. The man's face softened, his teeth gleamed through his yellow beard, and Gaius smiled in answer.

After what seemed to Gaius unending talk, the Council was at last dismissed, and the boy walked beside his father through the crowded town to the monastery. In open-faced booths along the sides of the streets, they passed men working at every kind of trade—potters, carpenters, tinsmiths, shoemakers, weavers, tailors.

In the market place, stalls held fruit, grains, and vegetables for sale. Such produce was brought in from the country by pack-horse, or cart, or in barges moving slowly along the winding, shallow river. So many people, all busy at their own affairs, talking, laughing, bargaining! Didn't they know of the danger that was near? Were they as careless as he, Gaius, had been only the day before? Gaius lifted his head as he walked. He felt, somehow, that he must have grown taller in that short space of time, because he surely felt many years older!

At the guest-house he learned that his mother and the house servants would remain in the city until his father and old Bleddoe went back to the villa. They would soon return to town with word of whether or not the Northmen had reached Gaius's house before the soldiers came. While his mother and father talked of their plans, Gaius told Father Paul what he had heard at the Council meeting.

The priest nodded when Gaius had finished. "Perhaps, after all, this is the beginning, and not the end that I had feared," he said. "Briton and Roman learned at last to live in this land together. Why not Angle and Saxon too?"

A *Blackbird Sings*

The boy in the next story lived about three hundred years after Gaius. The story tells things that happened in the country that is now called France. The people who ruled there were a branch of the German race, called Franks. These Franks had fought against the Romans and had driven them from Gaul. Gaul was the name for almost the whole of the country that we now know as Western Europe. Gaul, like Britain, had once been a part of the great Roman Empire.

The people in Gaul established the Kingdom of the Franks. About 250 years after the Franks had conquered the Romans, a wise man called Charlemagne[1] (Charles the Great) became King of the Franks. He wanted his people taught to read and write. He wished them to be as learned as the Romans had been in the days when Rome was strong and admired. Charlemagne was also a great soldier. He conquered and ruled many tribes and peoples. Many years after his death the empire which he ruled so well was divided into several small countries.

In the following story you will find out how some of the Franks lived and what kind of ruler Charlemagne was.

1. Pronounced *Sharlemane.*

EVEN under the green shade of the fruit trees, it was hot in the monastery garden. And still Brother Matthew's thin, whining voice droned on and on. The boys, seated in a half-circle about their teacher, nodded drowsily. Although all were working at the same task—copying Brother Matthew's words upon their wax tablets—they were divided into two separate groups. Those who sat upon the wooden benches wore bright-colored, finely made tunics of wool or embroidered linen, long hose banded with garters, and leather shoes. They were boys of noble birth. Those seated on the ground at the monk's feet wore rough dress of the common people and their legs and feet were bare. They were sons of peasants.

Remy was seated among his peasant companions on the grass. He shifted a little to ease a cramped muscle and then glanced up just in time to see a foot in a fine leather shoe thrust out suddenly toward him. Before he could move, the foot had struck against the wax of his tablet. The whole of his afternoon's work was

16

smeared and spoiled by one kick!

Remy looked up into the mocking face of the foot's owner, the young Count Hugo. Hugo's tablets lay on the bench beside him. He had not bothered to write down what the Brother had been reading. Instead, he was whittling idly at a stick. The shavings lay on the grass to show for it. But then Hugo was nephew of the Lord Abbot himself, who was head of the whole great monastery. Brother Matthew would never dare to punish Hugo!

For a single instant Remy stared into the close-set eyes of the young count. The angry color rose in his own sun-burned face until it reached the roots of his fair hair. Suddenly he reached out, seized Hugo's foot, and gave it a quick upward shove. Over went Hugo in a heap of arms and legs into the bushes behind the bench!

There was a gasp from the peasant boys and a cry of rage from Hugo, as he struggled to get up again. Brother Matthew stopped his reading and looked up. Annoyance showed in his small, red-rimmed eyes. When he saw who had made the disturbance, his face changed quickly. "What happened, my Lord Hugo?" he asked with concern as he helped Hugo to the bench.

"Remy—the insolent low-born puppy!" gasped Hugo, who was covered with leaves and dirt. "Flogging's too good for him!"

Brother Matthew turned a severe look on Remy. The boy's direct blue eyes met his. "Did you do that, Remy?" asked the teacher.

"Yes, master, but..."

The man cut him short. "Don't add tales and lies to your fault! Shame upon you! You are always showing this sinful pride and sauciness, Remy. Now choose. Either humbly beg the young Count's pardon, or go to work in the kitchen scullery[1] for the rest of the day—work truly suited to your low breeding!"

Remy got slowly to his feet. Hugo sat back upon the bench and looked at him with a broad, expectant smile. The other young nobles waited and watched, some with scorn, others with pity. The peasant lads kept their eyes fixed upon the ground as though they did not like to see their friend's disgrace. Then Remy squared his shoulders, turned and walked up the path toward the kitchen. He had not lied, nor would he beg Hugo's pardon.

Remy walked steadily with his head high, but in his throat there was an almost unbearable ache. He went to the kitchen door where a kindly lay brother, the chief cook, looked into his flushed, rebellious face. "More trouble with my young lord and his pretty mates? Well, here in the scullery we be all humble folk—no gentles nor nobles among us! Come, take this pot and work out your anger upon its blackness. Use this rag, and plenty of scouring sand, for it needs it!"

Remy took the heavy pot and carried it down to the shore of the pond beside the monastery mill. The pot was covered thick with greasy soot and lined with burnt food, but Remy's heart was so full of pent-up anger that scrubbing at it seemed almost to bring him

1. The dishwashing room.

18

relief. And as he worked he thought back over this, his first year at the monastery school.

Only a year ago Father John, priest of the distant little village where Remy had lived all of his twelve years, had called Remy's father and mother to him and given them great news. Of all his pupils in the parish school, their son showed the most promise. It was he, Remy, who must go to the monastery to continue his studies. All this must be done in obedience to King Charlemagne's recent decree, or order, Father John told the surprised peasant parents.

When Charlemagne, King of the Franks, came to the throne, he found that the long years of warfare had almost destroyed the learning that had been so prized by the ancient Romans. Books were few and even the priests and the monks were poorly trained in reading the Latin language in which all of the books then were written. Fighting, hunting, and feasting filled the days of the nobles. The common people found little time for anything but hard work.

Charlemagne had determined to change all this. Therefore he sent out royal decrees that commanded every village priest to teach reading and writing to every boy, noble or common, who had the will and ability to learn. When the priest could teach the boys no more (because of his own lack of training), those most gifted would be sent to the higher schools that the King had established in the monasteries, the cathedrals, and the palaces of the bishops. There the boys were to be housed and fed free of charge. And, for the chosen few of greatest promise, there was, last of all, the school that Charlemagne had set up in his own Royal Palace at Aix.[1]

Led by Father John, Remy had arrived at the monastery gate just a year ago. How full of marvels the great monastery had seemed to the boy then! Here, within its high walls lived more people than Remy had ever seen before. In his own little village the huts had been built of mud and wattles[2] and the roofs thatched with straw. Even the village church had been built of rough timber. Here the abbey church was built of stone and it had a high roof and a carved, gilded altar. The Abbot's house, though of wood like the other buildings, was still a palace in itself. Remy learned which was the long dormitory where the monks and their pupils slept and the refectory where they ate; the great kitchens; the almonry, where food was given out each morning to the poor who came begging to the gates; the stables, gardens, orchards; the busy mill, the clacking mill wheel and the quiet pond; the workshops of all kinds. It was like a city where each one worked happily at his own task.

But most splendid of all to Remy, with his newly won knowledge of reading, seemed the library. It was truly a house of treasures! Here the monastery kept all its precious books—manuscripts written on parchment. Wisdom and beauty, stored up for ages past by ancient, wise, and holy men, were here in the library, ready and waiting for anyone who had the skill to read!

Every day from the library a book was carried into

1. Pronounced as if it were the word *aches*.
2. Interwoven twigs and branches.

the scriptorium, or writing room. There one of the older monks read aloud from the precious parchment. The young scribes, or writers, sat at the desks and copied each word carefully in the fine black letters that they had been taught to make. This, too, was part of Charlemagne's great plan to make sure that wherever there were no books, they might be supplied.

Only last week Brother Felix, the writing teacher, had picked up the wax tablets from Remy's hand and had praised his work. Soon, he had said, Remy might be given pen and ink-pot, and might take his place among the copyists. Soon, but not until he had perfected his writing skill. The King had expressly urged that the copying be done by able and skillful writers, not "by careless and heedless boys"—so that there would be no errors in the books that were to be read by people not yet born.

Remembering this brought Remy's mind back to the scene in the garden with the young Count Hugo. He frowned again and worked with fresh energy at the sooty pot. Father John, that good and simple man, had not understood all that went on inside these monastery walls! He had told Remy that here hard work and honest ability would be the only measures of a boy's worth. He had said that here, as nowhere else, boys of low birth, such as he, would be equal with any warrior chief's or nobleman's son—"as it is in the Kingdom of Heaven"! Father John had even said that he, Remy, might be chosen to go from the monastery to the Royal Palace School at Aix! Remy's heart had beaten fast at the thought.

Well, Remy knew better now! In a month or less the Lord Abbot would go through the pretense of deciding which of his pupils was the most worthy of the honor, and already Hugo was boasting that it would be he!

"Aix—it's the wonder of the age!" Hugo had said. "The great new palace, and the hot pools where the King swims, and the great cathedral that he is building! Men come there from all corners of the earth. They bring riches and treasures past all belief! Why, the mighty Caliph of Bagdad, Haroun al Raschid, has sent a huge mountain of a beast called an elephant! He sent it as a gift to Charlemagne. It walks the streets, they say, for all the folk to see, carrying a dozen men upon its back!"

"As for me, why should I bend my neck over a desk? I shall spend a few years at the Palace attending the young princes, hunting in the Royal deer park. Then a countship or a good, rich abbey will be mine for the rest of my life! My father has only to ask for what he wishes from the King. Was it for holiness or or learning that my uncle got his post here as Abbot from Charlemagne's father, King Pippin? No, it was because my father asked it of him as a reward for his service in war, not for clerkly skill with a pen!"

Remy had no hope of any such honor as that of becoming an abbot! No, he knew well that such things were only for those of high birth. But to see Aix and to go to the Palace School, the source and spring of all learning in this thirsty Frankish land! That was different. That was something he wanted with his whole being. In his heart Remy knew that he was better fitted for it than the arrogant Hugo whose mind worked so slowly.

There in the Royal Palace at Aix King Charlemagne had gathered into his school the wisest and most learned men to be found in all the world! From far-away England came the noble Alcuin of Northumbria to be the chief of the school. From Spain came the poet Theodulf. From the famed monastery of Monte Cassino in Italy came Paul the Deacon, and from another part of the same land came Peter of Pisa. There in the Palace, these men taught. Charles himself, the unconquered King of the Franks, was himself a pupil! Charlemagne, ruler and warrior though he was, found his greatest pleasure in the study of the "Seven Liberal Arts" which were listed as grammar, rhetoric, dialectics, music, arithmetic, geometry, and astronomy. With his gentle Queen Liutgard, and his royal sister, his courtiers and councilors, his cousins, his sons and daughters, as well as those gifted youths who had been sent to the school from all over the land, the King listened to the lectures and took part in the discussions.

All these things Father John had told Remy. They had excited the boy's thoughts and had made him hope for many things. How hard he had studied at first! He had practiced his writing on the wax tablets long after the rest of the class was dismissed. Long hours he spent in the library reading the manuscripts until the sunset light faded and he could see no more. He had learned every note and every word of every song by heart!

23

The masters seemed pleased at first. They had praised his eagerness and industry. But when, one day, he had told Brother Matthew of his hope to go to the Palace School, the monk had raised his eyebrows. "Cast out such foolish, pridefull thoughts, my son!" he had said in a shocked voice. "Humble yourself and be content to serve well in the station to which you were born."

And after that it seemed to Remy that Brother Matthew had become more severe with him, as though to punish him for daring to raise his hopes so high.

The singing teacher alone, Brother Michael, was Remy's constant friend. A small, merry-faced old man, he had come walking up to the gate of the monastery soon after Remy's arrival. He had been dressed in a robe and cowl of undyed wool. A leather knapsak was on his back and a staff in his hand. From distant Ireland he had come on a pilgrimage, and the dust of many lands and cities was on his sandlaled feet.

For all his great learning—the monasteries of Ireland were famous centers of knowledge—Brother Michael was a simple, good-natured man whose greatest skill and interest was music. The Abbot had been glad to put him in charge of the singing class of his school.

As Brother Michael had found Remy's voice to be sweet and true, he was giving him special training. Nor was this training only in formal chants of the Church. Brother Michael knew many songs of his own land, old songs of the people. Their tunes haunted Remy even in his sleep, and their words made pictures in his mind of green islands far in the west; of orchards where white blossums hung from silver boughs, blossums that never faded, never fell; of tall warriors who drove chariots of shining bronze over the dark, wet sand of the ocean beach, who raced the wild horses of the sea!

Now, as Remy's thoughts were being carried far away by the words of such a song, he heard a sound that brought him to his feet. With scouring cloth in one hand and pot in the other, he stood listening. It was the sound of a trumpet blown at the main gateway of the monastery, the great gate that never was opened except for visitors of the highest rank. Immediately after the sound came such a stir and bustle as Remy had never heard before in the quiet monastery.

The gatekeeper's son, his face crimson with excitement, ran along the path toward the Abbot's house. As he ran he shouted back the news over his shoulder to Remy. "The King—King Charles and his train—are at the gate! I'm sent to tell the Lord Abbot!"

Charlemagne! Charlemagne here? Remy ran as fast as he could to the gate. He arrived just as it swung wide on its creaking, rusty hinges. Then in rode a company of armed and mounted men. At their head was a powerful, commanding figure on a prancing horse, a figure that could be no one else in all the wide world but Charlemagne himself! At first Remy hardly dared to look, but when he did it was to see blue eyes in a broad, high-colored face. Those eyes were crinkled in laughter and they smiled directly down upon Remy for an instant before the procession passed on.

Remy turned. Brother Michael stood there in the group beside him. "He smiled—he smiled—the King smiled at me!" stammered Remy, hardly able to believe what he had seen.

"And who wouldn't, covered as you are with soot from that pot you hold in your hand? You look more like a grinning blackamoor than a Christian—the wonder is that he did not laugh aloud!" chuckled the old monk. "Now go wash yourself, my boy. Unless I mistake, it's not just for his dinner that our King is paying us the honor of this sudden visit!"

Much crestfallen, and wondering what Brother Michael might meen by his last remark, Remy hurried back to the mill pond. He leaned over the edge to look at himself in the mirror made by the still water. He was indeed black with soot! He washed as well as he could, using the sand to scour himself until he all but took the skin off with the dirt.

Climbing back up the bank again, he met one of his classmates named Hilary. With a scared face Hilary was hurrying toward the dormitory. "I'm sent to call all the boys," he said. "We are to go to the Abbot's Hall, not only the young nobles but the rest of us as well. They say that we are to recite before the King!"

It was a crowd of pale, wide-eyed boys who filed into the Abbot's great hall. A strange man in churchman's clothes was there waiting for them. He gave out tablets to each boy. "Write a poem or essay of your own composition," he said. "These you are to read before the King when he comes, and thus you will show him how well you have studied."

The masters, Remy saw, looked almost as terrified as the boys. Their pupils were to recite before the

King, and they had no chance to prepare them! Brother Matthew chewed his fingernails and Brother Felix twisted the cord of his robe round and round until he made knots in it. Only Brother Michael seemed calm and serene. He looked out of the high window at the clouds sailing in the blue sky and he hummed a tune beneath his breath. And when he saw Remy's frightened stare upon him, he closed one eye gently, but unmistakably!

Then the hall was quiet except for the soft sound of writing and an occasional deep-drawn breath from one of the hard-working young scribes. Somehow the time passed. The churchman spoke to a gaily dressed Royal page who stood waiting at the door. In a few moments footsteps echoed on the stone floor of the passage. The door was flung open. Two armed soldiers entered and stood motionless, holding back the heavy curtain. The boys dropped to their knees as the tall, burly figure of the King entered the hall.

The King was dressed very much like his attendants. He wore a tunic of fringed silk, long stockings fastened by crossed bands, leather riding boots, and a cloak of fine blue wool. The long sword that hung by his side had a hilt of gold; the belt that held it was woven of gold threads and the buckle of his cloak was gold, and jeweled. He walked lightly for so large a man, and so rapidly up the aisle between the rows of boys that the plumb old Abbot, hurrying to keep up with him, breathed hard. When the Abbot turned, the boys saw that his face was splotched and red, his eyes anxious.

Charlemagne's expression, too, had changed from the smile he wore when he rode through the gate. Had something in the monastery displeased the King, wondered Remy, as he looked up at the frowning brows above the keen eyes and the stern expression of the bearded mouth?

Grim indeed grew the King's face as the young nobles, one by one, recited their compositions to him. Remy squirmed with shame and pity for all of them, even for Hugo, as he listened to them stutter and stumble through the reading of what were, in truth, poor attempts at good writing. Charlemagne moved impatiently in his chair when the last was finished. "Well, what of the others, those lads there? he asked. "Surely they cannot do worse, my Lord Abbot?"

Some of the peasant boys, frightened by the King's angry frown, stammered and halted too. But as a whole they made a good showing, far better than had the entire group of noble boys. Gradually Charlenagne's frown went away and he nodded with pleasure when the peasant boys had finished. He started to rise, then settled back in his chair again. "What of music?" he asked. "In my decrees I wrote urgently that you give due thought to the teaching of music. It is a way of worship that is most pleasing to Heaven, of that I am sure."

Brother Michael stepped forward. One look at his calm, cheerful face gave the boys new confidence. The young voices sounded fresh and clear as they chanted for the King the verses of the ancient Latin lymn *Veni Creator Spiritus*, written by Pope Gregory the Great. The King leaned back in his seat, relaxed and smiling; the fingers of one big, muscular hand marked the time on the arm of his chair.

"There is one voice that pleases me greatly," said Charlemagne, when the last not had faded. "Let him sing alone—that boy there in the front row."

Remy felt his knees begin to shake as he stepped forward. "What shall I sing?" he asked Brother Michael.

"I have taught the lad a song. The words are new and very pious and pleasing, but the tune is an old air of my people. It is called 'The Scribe,' " said Brother Michael.

"Good." Charlemagne nodded.

For a moment Remy's throat felt tight and dry, and it seemed as though no sound could possibly come out of it. But then he saw Brother Michael's kind, bright eyes upon him, saw his hand lifted up to mark the time. Suddenly his fear disappeared. He raised his head and began to sing.

> The trees like a hedge surround me
>   And a blackbird sings to me
> And on my book, and around me
>   The birds spill melody.
>
> From the topmost bough of the bushes falls
>   The gray-frock cuckoos' glee
> Oh it's good to write in the dear Lord's sight
>   Under the greenwood tree.[1]

1. From p. 186, Allen & Jones, *The Romanesque Lyric.*

"Good!" The King's broad, hearty smile was a warming sight to see. He stood up and turned to the group of peasant boys. "I thank you, my sons," he said, "for the effort with which you have followed my commands. Only go on as you have and I will reward you well. You shall be honorable in my eyes, and some of you, I know, will win splendid bishoprics and abbacies."

Then he turned about. His face grew stern and it seemed to Remy that his voice had a harsh, angry tone. "As for you, young nobles! You dainty and beautiful youths, who have thought that because of your high birth and your position you could despise my orders and give no thought to my power! You have neglected your studies and given yourselves to idleness. By the King of Heaven, *I* care nothing for your noble birth or your handsome faces! Know this for certain; unless you give earnest heed to your studies and make up for all you haven't done, never look for favor from the hand of King Charles!"

For a moment no one in the hall dared to breathe. The Abbot's red face was pale and he glared across the room at his nephew, the unlucky Hugo who had so openly disgraced himself beyond all hope of help from the King!

Charlemagne spoke again, more gently. "Come here, lad, you that sang." Remy stepped forward and knelt at the King's feet. "Young master blackbird, your singing pleased me." He put his hand kindly on the boy's bright yellow hair and suddenly chuckled. "You were a blackbird in truth, earlier this afternoon. It must have been a task to remove all that soot! Now listen. I have need of good voices among my pages. Will you come to the Palace at Aix and sing for me there while you continue your studies at the Palace School?"

Remy's mouth fell open. He hardly dared to believe the words that he had heard. Then, although he tried, he could not speak. He could only nod dumbly while, in spite of all he could do to keep them back, tears gathered in his eyes.

"Well, so let it be, then. And you, reverend Brother Musician, will you come and teach my pages to sing the songs of your country? Let these two be sent to Aix, my Lord Abbot, and speedily. I myself am traveling on to the seacoast to order the building of ships, for the Vikings are attacking my shores too boldly. But when I return I have work for a musician. I wish the old songs, yes, the old heathen songs of our people gathered together and written down before they are all forgotten. If it is good and right to keep the poetry of the ancient Romans, though they were not Christians, surely we should do the same for that of our own forefathers."

Then with his long swift stride he left the hall, the guards followed, and the curtains swung into place behind him.

Now that the King was gone, the boys crowded around Remy. It made him happy to see their pleasure in his good fortune. Even some of the young nobles, their faces a little sheepish, told him that they knew he had won what he deserved.

Brother Michael lingered behind the other masters and Remy hurried to his side. They stepped out into the afternoon's glowing sunshine, and as they walked the old man put an arm about the boy's shoulder. "It's off to the grand city of Aix, then," he said. "There you will find more things than the learning of saints spread before you. The King's favor and your own good heart can carry you far, my boy. But promise me never go too far to hear beauty in the blackbird's song from the country hedge!"

And Remy promised.

The People Remembered

YOU WILL REMEMBER that in the story about Gaius, the Roman-British Council decided to ask the Angle and the Saxon chiefs to help protect the people of Britain from the warriors of the North. In return for this help the Angles and Saxons were to be given land in Kent.

Large numbers of Saxons came and the Northern invaders were kept out of Britain. However, so many Saxons came that they asked for more land than the British were willing to give. If they were not given more land, the Saxons said, they would fight for it. And fight for it they did. For many years Britons were enemies of the Angles and Saxons. As the Angles and Saxons were stronger and more numerous, they finally conquered and drove out almost all of the Britons from the southern part of the Island. After many, many years this country was called Angleland, and the people who lived in England were known as Anglo-Saxons. In time, many of them became Christians.

At about the time the story you are going to read takes place, the Anglo-Saxon people themselves were attacked by Northern pirates. This time the warriors were Danes who sailed the seas in great fleets of ships. These Vikings, as they are called, were bold, daring, and active men. Time after time they sailed to England and there destroyed homes, villages, and churches, and killed many people. To their Danish homes they took all the valuable things they could find. After a while the Danes decided to drive all the English people from England and to make new homes there. Ethelred, King of England, and his army fought bravely with the Danes. But it was his younger brother Alfred who finally conquered the Northern enemies and forced them to make peace.

It is about Alfred and an English boy named Cedric that you will read in this story. Cedric lived about four hundred years after Gaius, who, you will remember, also lived in England.

NORSE SHIP.

CEDRIC was tired and hungry. He could tell by the way the sun shown down through the trees that it was now well past noon. Since dawn he had been hunting through brush and thorns for a pig that had strayed away from his father's herd of poor, lean swine. Cedric feared for a time that it had been caught by a wolf or some other of the wild animals that roamed the forest at night. But at last he had found the pig, and now he was driving it back to the clearing where the peasant village stood.

The people called it their village, but it was really nothing but a group of poorly made huts. Some were mud and wattle houses; others were no more than caves dug out of the soft dirt of a sloping bank.

Cedric was ten years old, and he could remember that this had not always been his home. Once he had lived in the pleasant, sunny valley beyond the forest. The valley was filled with green orchards and fertile fields. He could even remember how the abbey church and the other buildings of the monastery had towered above the low thatched cottages of the peasants. He remembered, too, the lovely sound of the abbey bells as they rang out in the morning and at sunset.

But then the Northmen had come—the cruel Danish Vikings. Before the fury of the Danes' attack those of the Saxon peasants who escaped alive fled to the depths of this dark, marshy wood. Here, terrified, they watched their cottages, the buildings of the monastery, the wooden roof of the stone-built abbey church itself, all go up in one great sheet of flame. Even the grain that stood ripe in the field waiting for harvest had been burned. The orchard trees were cut down and destroyed. The helpless peasants, seeing the ruin, had thought fearfully of the long, hungry winter that lay ahead.

Many of them had not lived through that first winter, Cedric remembered with a shudder. But now it was not so bad. The people had learned to make a sort of living in the forest. They dug edible roots, gathered and dried berries and wild fruit. Like squirrels, they stored nuts and acorns. They had found a few of the surviving cattle, sheep, and swine, and built shelters to protect them against the beasts of prey. Sometimes, too, they were lucky enough to spear or trap wild game for food. Best of all, no pitiless Northman had yet found the way through the secret paths to their hiding place.

Now, as Cedric drew nearer to his home, a sound of voices reached his ears. What could it mean? Why had the villagers gathered together at this time of day? He hurried to drive the stray pig into the brush enclosure that served for a pen, and ran to see what it was all about.

In the open space in the center of the group of huts the people were gathered around a man. This stranger looked as Cedric remembered the monks of the abbey. Instead of tattered rags or garments made of skins, such as the villagers wore, he was dressed in a long robe of woolen cloth tied in at the waist with a knotted cord. His robe and his sandaled feet were gray with dust. He had walked far.

"I tell you it is true!" Cedric heard him say. "There has been a great battle fought in the North, at a place called Edghill. Alfred our King has met the Danish heathen and has completely conquered them. All this happened more than a month ago." He looked round at the staring, silent peasants. "Guthrum, the Danish leader, has given himself as prisoner with all his captains Can you not understand what that means? Peace has come at last. You can leave this swamp and go back to your homes once more!"

In the crowd Cedric saw his own father and looked

to see what he would say. He was a thin, stooping man with a beard that was streaked with gray. Wulf was his name, and he was shaking his head gloomily. "The Danes are many. Conquer one army and another appears," he said. "So it has always been since they first came across the sea in their long, dragon ships!"

And a woman in the crowd nodded. "Here in this wood we may be hungry, but at least we are safe from the Danes if they return!" she said.

"This time it is different!" The monk's voice was very earnest. "You have only to look out into the open beyond your wood, and you will see that the great road through the valley is already travelled as in olden days. Merchants and peddlers are carrying their wares as before. Surely this is a proof of peace!"

"It may be. But we have been hunted and harried so long..." began Wulf.

"Alfred the King has forced the Danes to sign a treaty promising that they will abide by his laws," said the monk. "He himself has proclaimed the peace!"

"The Danes keep no treaties," said Wulf. "If we go back to our fields and rebuild our homes, they will only come again and destroy all that we own, as before. Still—if the King has proclaimed peace—Alfred is a truth-teller. We all know that..." he hesitated and other anxious and uncertain voices joined in.

Cedric did not wait to hear any more. He turned, and his bare, brown feet seemed scarcely to touch the ground as he ran. If there *were* travelers on the great highway that ran north and south, then the news that the monk brought must be true. He would go see for himself!

At the edge of the forest, before he left its safe, protecting shadows, he stopped for a moment. Cedric had lived for so many of his ten years in the forest that he had learned some of the habits of the small wild creatures whose home he shared. There was danger in an open space. Crossing it took courage!

But he could not see the road from here. Ahead of him, on a little hill, stood the ruins of the abbey church. The peasant village and the other monastery buildings were now only heaps of ashes and charred timbers, overgrown with weeds and grass. But the church, built of stone, had resisted the fire. Some of the huge pillars that were part of the wall, and a few rounded arches still stood upright. The stones were blackened where the fire had scorched them, and they were streaked with the winter rains. Cedric knew that from where those pillars stood he could see all of the road that crossed the valley. Moreover, the tumbled stones would be a hiding place for him if it should happen that the monk's news was not true, and the cruel Danes were still roaming the land.

Across the open space Cedric ran in one breathless dash. Quickly he climbed the rough stones of the broken wall until he could overlook the valley. Here he could see the white line of the road as it was marked across the green countryside. Yes, people were moving along it, not only toward the south, but northward as well! Surely it *must* be true that the Danes were conquered! Otherwise, how would any Englishman dare to drive a loaded ox-cart, such as Cedric could plainly see lumbering along the road, straight toward the dangerous border of the country which the Danes had held?

Most of those coming from the north were armed men. Cedric could see the metal of their helmets and spear points as it shown in the sun. They moved slowly. Some of them seemed very weary, others limped as though they had severe wounds. But he saw in them none of the furious speed of men fleeing before an enemy. Instead these men seemed to be going slowly and steadily back to their homes after work that was over and done.

A group of these soldiers were resting and eating in the shade of a tree. Was that bread they were eating? Real bread? From this distance Cedric could not be sure, but the thought of brown, crusty, oaten bread made his mouth water, and made him remember also how long it was since he had tasted food. And as for bread—he could scarcely recall when he had eaten bread last, but he had not forgotten the flavor!

Then a cloud of dust appeared suddenly where the road crossed the border of the valley. Cedric saw a troop of mounted men come riding swiftly down the hill. As he watched, the soldiers under the tree jumped to their feet. They waved their arms and shouted and cheered as the riders past. Cedric tried to see who these newcomers might be. But the dust was thick and the sun blinded his eyes.

Abruptly the horsemen turned off the road. They were riding straight toward the ruins of the abbey! Cedric was frightened, but his curiosity was stronger than his fear. He stayed, clinging like a lizard to the wall. Just below him, the leader of the mounted troop pulled his horse to a stop.

"So this is all that the Danes left of our fair abbey!" said a deep, pleasant voice. "I have spent many a night here with the reverend brothers of this order and have knelt to hear Mass where this grass is growing out of the pavement! There was a well of sweet water just outside the church door. Surely *that* cannot be gone, too!"

"Here it is my Lord King!" one of the riders said as he swung from his saddle to the ground. "The curbing is broken, but the water looks clear enough."

"My Lord King!" Would a king wear no other sign of rank than a narrow golden band around his helmet? Was this young man in the plain armor of chain mail Alfred the King himself? Cedric's foot slipped and dislodged a bit of stone from the wall. It fell, almost striking the King's horse. Alfred looked up, and Cedric found himself staring directly down into wide-spaced eyes and a tired, worn face.

"Well, boy, and what are you doing up there?" asked the King after his first instant of surprise.

"I was only looking..." began Cedric. Then his shyness overcame him completely and he could say no more.

"Looking for what?" the King smiled. His smile was so kind that Cedric had courage to go ahead.

"A man—a traveling monk—said that the Danes had been beaten. And when we would not believe him, he said that, as proof, travelers were already using the road again. I was looking to see."

"And have you seen them?"

"Yes, I can see travelers on the road."

"And is that proof enough for you that peace is here?"

"I—I think so. But my father..."

"Well, what of your father? Can he not believe his eyes?" asked the King, as Cedric hesitated again.

"My father says that the Danes keep no treaties, and that if we rebuild our houses and replant our fields, the Danes will only come again and destroy everything as before. But if *you* should say that peace is here for good, I think that he would believe you, because he says that all men know that you speak the truth!"

There was a stir among the riders as the stern warriors looked at one another and smiled. The color that rose in the King's tired face made it suddenly young again.

"Where is your father, boy?" asked Alfred.

"All of our people are living in the forest," said Cedric.

"Then I will go into the forest and speak to them myself," said the King. "Come, climb down from your perch and ride here in front of me. There is room for two rascals of your size—I know, for I have carried my own little son thus." He urged his great black horse close to the wall and Cedric, in a daze of wonder, obeyed.

Seated on the King's war horse, with the King's strong arm holding him firmly, Cedric forgot hunger and weariness. Proudly and eagerly he guided the soldiers through the dimly marked paths of the forest. The sound of the horses brought the frightened peasants out of their huts. They stared with wonder and awe. Their King, Alfred, King of the West Saxons, here in their forest? When they were all gathered about him, the King spoke.

"I have come to bring you news," he said. "Great news for all our nation. Guthrum, the Dane, has yielded. What is more, he and his chiefs have submitted humbly to Christian baptism. They have admitted defeat and have withdrawn again into their own lands beyond the rivers Thames and Lea and Ouse.[1] Those are the borders set by the treaty signed only this week at Wedmore. It is from there that I have ridden today.

"I have come here into this wood to find you, because I want you to know that this is true. This boy says that you will believe me if I tell you myself. I wish that I could speak thus face to face with all our Saxon folk, because from this day forward I need every man's help, as I have never needed it before."

The King paused, and the peasants turned to one another with troubled, wondering faces. Then Wulf the swineherd stepped forward. "All of the men here are either old, or sick. Our strong young men have gone with your armies long before this, King Alfred. What help can we give you, folk such as we?"

"I will tell you," answered the King. "You can give me two great things, your faith and your trust. I have many hard tasks before me. First and foremost,

1. Pronounced *Tems, Lee, Ooz*.

as you know, I must make certain of this peace. Treaties are no stronger than the pledged words of those who sign them. Therefore I am building forts along our borders, and in them men will keep watch day and night against any treachery from those who were lately our enemies. And I am building great ships to guard our coast from attack by sea. All this I must do, to keep this peace that we have won.

"But what is all this for? Why must soldiers of mine still carry their heavy arms and these seamen brave fogs and reefs and stormy seas? Why? So that you too can play your parts in the rebuilding of our poor broken land. For I tell you that this fertile earth of ours is not worth the blood that has been shed for it, unless you men and women take up your tasks again. You, and you alone, can make the earth bring forth grain and bear fruit as before. You have the skill, learned from your father's before you, to tend your flocks and herds, milk your cows, and shear your sheep. You have the power in your hands to bring plenty back to the land when the fighting men have bought the peace."

He paused again, and Cedric saw the peasants look at one another. This time they nodded in agreement. This was right, this was good sense. They could understand what King Alfred was saying! Bent shoulders straightened and heads lifted as the King continued.

"Peace and plenty I want for my land," the King said. "And something else too. I passed a blackened ruin as I rode here—the ruin of the abbey that once stood in your valley. The heathen Danes have destroyed

43

churches and holy places all through the country. They must be rebuilt. But far harder than piling together stones and mortar will be the rebuilding of what those places contained. Fire has destroyed the libraries of learned books; the sword has killed the learned men. In all our Saxon land there are pitifully few left who can do so much as read, to say nothing of teaching reading to others.

"But it is my resolve"—Cedric saw the King's eyes flash as he spoke—"to establish so many schools throughout my kingdom that before my reign is ended every youth who wishes to do so can learn reading and writing, and every parish church can have its own copy of the Holy Book. Yes, not in Latin, merely, but in our English tongue as well, so that the humblest of my people can understand what that Book contains!

"Much heavy toil lies ahead before all this can be accomplished, hard work for each of us—King and churchman, soldier and peasant. Each one of us must take up his task with good faith and a strong heart. The soldier needs the bread that the farmer can grow, and the farmer needs the peace that the soldier can guard for him. Both need just laws from their King, and all need the wisdom and guidance of the Church.

"Now I must go, for we have far to ride before night comes." With a firm hand the King helped Cedric down from his horse to the ground. Then he lifted his rein, but checked his horse for a moment more. "My own boy has such yellow hair. It seems long to me since I saw him last." He looked once again into the upturned faces of the peasants. "You have heard what

44

I came to say. Will you remember?"

"We will remember!" cried Cedric and his father and all the rest in one great breath.

Alfred turned his horse. With his followers he rode away between the tall trunks of the trees. A long ray of sunlight slanted down through the branches and shown for a moment upon the golden circle around Alfred's helmet. Then the forest shadows closed in upon him and his soldiers.

Even after he was gone from their sight, the peasants stood looking after him and listening to the sound of his horse's hoofs. Nor did any one of them forget his words.

Hail Normansland!

THE STORY which you are to read now tells about a girl and a boy who lived in Norway. You will remember that in the story, "The Blackbird Sings," you were told that Charlemagne was traveling to the seaports of France. There he was going to build ships that were to be used in fighting the Vikings (Norwegians and Danes) who came from the northern part of Europe.

Who were these "Northmen," these Vikings, of whom you have read so often? The name Viking comes from the word "vik," or bay. It was among the many bays and inlets along the coasts of Norway and Denmark that they lived. Because their homes were so close to the sea, they learned sooner than the rest of the Europeans how to build strong, swift boats. They became skillful and daring sailors. Vikings in their long, narrow "serpent ships" made voyages as far west as Iceland, Greenland, and North America, as far south as Africa, as far east as Constantinople. They even took some of their ships up the rivers into Russia.

Sometimes they voyaged for peaceful trading, but more often they went to make warlike raids on their neighbors. In the next story you will read about what happened when these Vikings, after many raids in France, became stronger than the Franks.

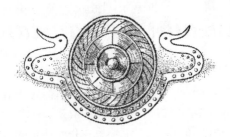

A BRIGHT morning sun scattered rainbow-colored sparkles all over the green grass on the dewy hillside. It danced on the tiny waves that rippled on the shore below. In from the sea beyond the bay came a fresh wind that lifted Astrid's yellow hair from her forehead. It lifted her hair, but it did not smooth her frown as she looked down on the beach where her older brother, twelve-year-old Thord, worked in one of the smallest of the boats that were pulled up beside the stone wharf.

Astrid stood in the doorway of the largest of a group of log houses built on the steep hillside. Behind her, inside the great hall, she could hear the voices of her mother's maid-servants as they chattered while they worked. She could hear, too, the regular thumping noise of the great wooden loom at which her mother, the Lady Ingeborg, was weaving fine linen cloth. For such cloth she was famous throughout this part of Norway.

From the nearest of the other buildings, the cooking house, came the sound of more voices. Smoke, rising from the smoke-hole in the roof, floated away upon the light breeze. Beyond the cooking house were the great barns. Astrid could hear the beat of flails upon the wooden floors as her father's farm workers threshed out the grain.

It was a fair and cheerful scene on that bright September morning, but Astrid looked out upon it with resentment clouding her blue eyes. She turned at a sound behind her; her mother had stopped her weaving to come and stand at her side in the open doorway. "What troubles you, little daughter?" she asked. The sun glowed on the Lady Ingeborg's gown of finely woven scarlet cloth and on her thick fair hair bound in two braids. These braids were so long that she had tucked them inside her embroidered belt to keep them out of her way.

"Thord promised me yesterday that he would take me fishing beyond the island in his boat!" said Astrid. "But this morning he says that I cannot go. He says that I am only a girl, and that girls should stay at home! He is taking Barni in my place!" Her eyes filled, but she blinked the tears back angrily. "Mother, I wish I were a boy! Before Thord was as old as I am now, he had been with father on two trading cruises, and he is boasting now that he will sail with father on his next Viking voyage in the spring. And *I* have never seen beyond these bays and islands where I was born!"

The Lady Ingeborg smiled gently down into the small, flushed face. "You have been thinking of what the old beggar woman told you—the one who said that she had second sight. The old woman said that you would travel far, but that was not until she learned that such was your dearest wish! She had her eyes on the silver coin you gave her—not on the future, I am afraid! Do not believe too much in such things, Astrid." She paused, then continued more gaily. "But in a few years your time will come to marry. Perhaps your husband, whoever he may be, will take you in his long ship to a far country—too far, and too soon for my liking! Now, while you are a little maid, be content to stay here in your father's hall!"

Such a future was too distant to make Astrid feel less unhappy. She started to reply, but paused as a man appeared round the corner of the house with a long haying fork across his shoulder. The newcomer was Eirik, the overseer, or manager, of the farm. Eirik was the Lady Ingeborg's chief aid while her husband, Jarl Helge, was sailing far away in his long ship. Eirik was a freeman, not a thrall (a slave captured in war or bought for a price), as were most of the men who farmed the land. His hair and beard were grizzled and his face was a deep brown color, but his eyes held a merry twinkle that Astrid loved.

"Good morning, Eirik," said the Lady Ingeborg to the old man. "What do you think of a little maid who, on a fine morning such as this, complains that she cannot go avoyaging like her brother?"

"Well," said Eirik, "if it's voyaging that she wants, let her come with us. We're rowing across to the island to bring back the hay that has been drying there. Young master Thord has given up his fishing trip to come with us. It may not be much of a cruise, but it would be a beginning!"

Astrid's face had lighted eagerly at Eirik's first words, but the eagerness faded when she learned where the *voyage* was to end. However, she thought, it would be better than nothing. Astrid was active and strong for her ten years, and outdoor work was always more to her taste than sewing with the maids in the hall. "May I go, mother?" she asked.

"Yes, if you will promise to help, not merely play in the hay," said her mother. "Stop at the kitchen for food—you will need something if you are to be gone all day. And perhaps," she added, smiling, "if you look out to sea from the high rocks at the end of the island, you may be the first of us all to catch sight of your father's long dragon ship, returning home at last!"

At the kitchen a cooking maid wrapped bread and cheese in a clean white cloth for her. Then Astrid ran down the path to the water's edge. There the farm thralls were already loading their haying tools into the big, flat-bottomed barge that was to carry the hay back from the island. Thord looked surprised when Astrid told him that she was to go too. "Much help you'll be!" he said scornfully. But old Eirik made room for her beside him in the stern where he stood to hold the long steering oar.

As they moved out into the quiet water of the channel, Astrid turned in her place to look back. The many log buildings that made up their home stood out distinctly against the bright green of the grass and the darker green of the pine forest on the slope behind. From here, too, Astrid could see the waterfall that hung like a fine white veil against the rocky mountain wall. This waterfall she could not see from her home, but its deep, soft voice was always in her ears.

Astrid and Thord had the same fair hair and blue eyes as their mother. They were tall, and they held their heads high as children of a nobleman, or jarl, were expected to do. Both of them today wore smocks of coarsely woven linen. They were made alike except that Astrid's was much longer and fuller than her brother's. For best wear they had garments of fine, brilliantly dyed wool, or even of silk that was brought by traders from the distant East. But their clothing for every day was much the same as that worn by the thralls, with only an added touch of embroidery at neck or hem. Around Astrid's neck hung a necklace of golden beads. Thord wore an arm-band of the same bright metal.

Astrid new how important it was to her father, Jarl Helge, to get the crop of hay into his barns safely. In this far, Northern land, the snow fell early and lasted late into the spring. The winters were long and cruelly cold. Without barns stored full of hay and grain, the herds of cattle, the horses, the flocks of sheep, would starve before the grass grew to feed them in the spring. Jarl Helge was a bold sea-rover and a fierce fighter when he was on one of his Viking voyages, but at home he was a careful farmer. Before setting sail in his long dragon-prowed ship, he had made sure that his fields were plowed and planted with seed. When he returned, he would look to it that his barns and granaries were full.

"Do you think that there is a chance that we might see my father—that he will be coming home today?" Astrid asked of old Eirik.

"This day is as well as any. When Jarl Helge sailed on this Viking voyage, he said that he would return about the time of the last hay harvest," answered Eirik kindly.

The distance across to the island was short, and soon the barge's keel grated on the gravelly shore. A long-necked heron, that had been fishing for eels in the shallow water, rose with a hoarse croak and flapped heavily away. Thord scrambled out of the barge behind the men, and Astrid followed. Carried on the keen, salt ocean breeze was the sweet odor of sun-dried hay. A flock of gulls rose like a white cloud from the beach and circled and screamed above the children's heads. Their wings flashed against the blue of the sky.

The two children set to work with the men. They helped to lift the hay from the long racks that stretched across the fields. On these racks it had dried thoroughly in spite of the dampness of the sea fogs rolling in by night. When one of the carrying frames was piled high with hay, two of the strongest thralls carried it between them down to the barge that waited at the water's edge. The men sang as they worked. Their songs were timed to the rhythm of their labor.

They sang old songs, sagas of ancient chiefs and bold warriors of long ago that Astrid and Thord loved to hear. Christianity, with its message of gentleness and goodwill, had not yet reached this Northern land. Here the people still believed in the fierce Norse gods of war and revenge. So long as a man were true to his given word and loyal to his friends, he might be cruel and merciless to others and still be called a hero.

At first the work seemed like play, but as the sun rose higher in the sky, even the fresh wind from the sea failed to cool the children's hot faces. When old Eirik finally announced that midday had come, Astrid and Thord were both glad to rest their tired arms and aching backs.

The men flung themselves down to lie full length in the shade of a clump of white birches and red-berried rowan trees.

"Let's take our lunch to the top of the cliff," said Astrid.

"Mother and Eirik both said that if we looked from there we might see father's ship returning over the water."

"They were only joking," said Thord. "He has been gone since spring. There is no way of telling the day of his return." But as he, too, liked to climb the rocky headland, he followed Astrid as she started up the slope.

As they climbed, the meadow-grass gave way to flower-starred heather, and then to patches of gray granite rock. The few trees that grew here were twisted into strange shapes by the constant force of the sea wind. At last they reached the top of the headland. Here they could look out upon miles of rocky pine-grown shore and more miles of empty ocean where not even a porpoise broke the broad expanse of blue.

1. Pronounced *liken*. A moss-like plant that grows on rocks.

They sat to rest on a rock where gray lichen[1] had made patterns that were as lovely and fine as those that the Lady Ingeborg worked with her needle during the long winter days. Because he was the older, Thord divided the bread and cheese into two equal parts. The wind was cool and pleasant, and the crusty brown bread and savory cheese seemed to taste better than ever before.

"Which way would father's ship be coming from—if it *should* come now?" Astrid asked when her first hunger was satisfied.

"From the south. He went to join Jarl Ragnhild's son, Rolf the Walker, in his war with the Franks," said Thord. "The Frankish land lies far to the south. Rolf the Walker has a great fleet of long ships and an army of warriors. Already they have conquered many towns along the seacoast, and have sailed up the river Seine into the very center of the Frankish province of Neustria."

"If Rolf is a jarl's son, why do they call him the Walker? Doesn't he have a horse to ride by land as well as a ship by sea?"

"They call him that because he is so huge a man that few horses are strong enough to carry his weight," Thord told her. "He is a wise and crafty leader as well as a mighty fighter in battle. If they are still fighting in the south next year, I shall join him also, when I go with father on his spring Viking voyage."

"I wish I could go too," said Astrid, the cloud returning to her blue eyes.

"You? A girl on a Viking voyage!" Thord threw back his head and laughed aloud at such a thought.

"Well, perhaps not on a Viking voyage. But sometimes father sails for trade, not for battle. Why couldn't I go with him then? I should so love to see that flowery southern land, where the sun shines warmly even in midwinter!"

But Thord shook his head. "A girl who is a jarl's daughter stays in her father's house—until, of course, she marries. Then her husband takes her to his house, and she stays there. No, my little Astrid, your life lies here among these bays and islands of Norway, where you were born!"

Astrid had heard such words before, and yet she would not accept them meekly. She lifted her round chin and she answered. "If my father will not take me, nor you, nor my husband when I marry, then I shall sell my bracelets and my golden beads and buy a ship and go myself!" she said. "I have wished for it on every magic charm I know, and the second-sighted woman *told* me that my wish would come true! I shall see more of the world than you think, Thord!"

Thord was starting to reply when Astrid clutched him suddenly by the arm. "Look!" she cried, pointing. "Isn't that a ship just rounding the point yonder?"

Sure enough, as they watched, a great, square sail, filled to roundness by the wind, came into their view. The sail was striped in purple and red and black. Below it the sun glinted on the high prow that was carved to the likeness of a rearing dragon's head. "It's father's ship!" cried Astrid. "I know it is—I know the pattern of the sail, for I helped mother when she wove it on her great loom! It *is* father's ship!"

But Thord was already running back toward the meadow to spread the news. He jumped like a deer from rock to rock as he ran. For a moment more Astrid watched the long ship as it moved so swiftly over the blue water. Foam curled before it and its long white wake trailed behind. Along the side hung a row of bright-colored disks. These were the painted shields of the Viking warriors who sat along the benches inside the ship. In the stern Astrid saw the steersman, a tall figure whose gilded helmet glittered in the sun, while the wind blew his scarlet cloak. Surely that could be none other that her father, Jarl Helge himself!

Astrid waited no longer, but ran as fast as her feet would carry her to the shore where the haymakers were already climbing aboard the half-loaded hay barge. The return of the Jarl and his warriors from their long cruise meant holiday and feasting for the whole country for miles around!

The Viking ship rounded the island, followed the channel, and drew up at last beside the stone pier in the harbor. By this time everyone on the farm, from the Lady Ingeborg to the lowest thrall, was waiting to greet the returning warriors. Jarl Helge in his golden helmet and shirt of shining chain mail was the first to leap from his ship's deck to the shore. He gathered his wife and children into his strong arms. How glad they were to have him safe home again, after the long, dangerous voyage!

"Spread the news of our return far and wide!" the Jarl ordered. "Call our friends and neighbors to join us at our feast. Tell them we have returned with a great shipload of rich booty, and with greater news!"

The Lady Ingeborg hurried away to make ready for the feast that would honor he husband's return. Huge quarters of beef and mutton were set to roasting before open fires. Into the hall servingmen carried trestles and across them they laid the long table boards. Benches were set into place, and piled high with the thick, soft skins of bears and wolves to serve as cushions. Astrid helped the maidservants to scatter fresh green rushes over the hard-packed dirt floor; these gave out a sweet fragrance when walked upon.

The wooden walls of the hall were covered with the finest and gayest of woven and embroidered hangings. Then, when the hall was decorated to her liking, Lady Ingeborg gave the word for the thralls to carry in the high seat of the Jarl himself. They set it in its place at the longest table—this high seat, with its four tall carved and painted posts.

Astrid would have liked to stay close beside her father while he walked over his farm inspecting the work that had been done while he was away. But there was still much to prepare before the feast was ready. The Jarl and his warriors had asked to have the wooden bath-house made ready for them. Here huge fires were lit to heat the water and make the steam that would take the soreness and ache from their tired bodies. Already, too, guests were beginning to arrive by horse or by boat and were greeted at the door of the hall. All wished to hear of the Jarl's adventures, and to know what was this great news that he had brought.

To Astrid the most welcome of all the guests was Halfred the Skald, or singer. He rode up to the Jarl's door with his gilded harp slung upon his back. After the feasting he would play and sing there in the hall. Perhaps, thought Astrid, her heart beating fast, perhaps he would sing a new song. Perhaps he would sing one made up especially in honor of Jarl Helge to tell the tale of his voyage and his victories! Halfred was a famous skald. On his arms he wore the bracelets of the purest yellow gold that were given him by jarls and even kings because of their delight in his songs.

At last, just as the sun set, the feast was ready. The guests took their places at the long tables. Torches blazed smokily in iron brackets, and in the central fire-pit the burning scented pine wood helped to give out light. The fire glittered on the bright colors of the clothing worn by the men and women, on their jewel-set ornaments, and on the gold and silver plates, bowls and goblets, that decked the tables. These dishes were booty that the Jarl had captured on his raids. The serving men carried in great platters of freshly roasted meat, bread, sweetened cakes, fruit, and bowls of curded milk. The table boards almost bent beneath their weight!

Astrid wore her finest dress of bright blue silk stiff with gay embroidery, and her hair was smoothly combed and braided. Soon she would take her place beside her mother at the long table. But first she must fill the tall golden drinking horn and present it to her father, for that was her duty as daughter of the house.

Jarl Helge took the drinking horn from his daughter and held it while the servants passed up and down the long table to give each one of the Viking warriors and each of the guests a drinking horn. Then the Jarl rose to his feet. The hall was quiet, for everyone wanted to hear what he might have to say.

"Friends and neighbors, and you, my comrades, this is a glad day for me," he began. "It is a glad day, because I have returned from a successful voyage with much booty, and I have found that my farms have prospered and my wife and children are blooming with health. It is a glad day for me, but it is also a sad day, too, and I will tell you why. This is the last time that I shall gather my friends about me to a feast in this hall."

He paused. The warriors who had been the Jarl's companions nodded as though they understood, but the others looked at one another in surprise. A murmur rose among them.

"The last time, Jarl Helge?" asked one of his neighbors.

"Yes. This is the news that I have for you. You all know of the many years that we have made war in the Frankish land. There we take what we will of the riches that they are too weak to hold. You have heard of our victories this year. Now this is my news! At St. Claire on the Epte, Rolf the Walker signed a treaty with that unworthy descendant of Charlemagne, Charles the Simple, King of the Franks. Charles has acknowledged at last our right to the land that we have conquered with the sword—the whole of the province called Neustria. It is to be ours forever in return for our promise to keep peace with the King and to defend the land from other Northern raiders. And, in truth, after so many years of fighting, I, for one, shall be glad of peace."

"Glad of peace? Those sound like weakling Christian words!" cried a gruff-voiced, grizzled warrior from the end of a long table.

For a moment there was a startled silence in the hall. Heads turned in alarm to hear what angry answer the Jarl would make. But though his face grew grave, he did not speak angrily.

"Rolf the Walker, Ragnhild's son, is no weakling," he said. "Yet Rolf has promised the Frankish King to become a Christian. Those long-robed priests may be weak in battle, but their words have a strange and moving power. Their words can pierce through the strongest armor straight to a man's heart. But, as for me, I have made no such promise as yet, because I believe that a man should think long before deserting the god's of his fathers."

He looked around at his silent, attentive guests; then he continued once more. "This province that we have won has fertile soil. It is free from stones and is warmed by the sun long after this Norway of ours lies buried under drifts of snow. Rolf has divided the land among those who fought with him. To my share have fallen many rich acres of fields and forest along the river Seine.[1] That is why this is my last feast here. I have sold my lands and my house here in Norway to Olaf, who fought bravely at my side. Before the snow

1. Pronounced *Sane*.

flies again, I shall have sailed southward with my household, to build a new house there in the new land. It will be a fine house with a tall tower of stone, like those of the Frankish nobles, for my wife and my son and my blue-eyed little Astrid here!"

Jarl Helge reached out and drew Astrid into the circle of his arm. With the other he held the golden drinking horn high above his head. "Skoal!" he cried. "Hail to the new home of the Northmen—no longer Neustria, but Normansland!"

From the warriors in the hall rose an answering shout so loud that the smoky rafters shook with the sound. Astrid's high, triumphant cry joined in, but it was lost in the thunder of the men's voices. Was it only this morning, she thought, that Thord had told her that never, never would she see beyond the bays and islands of Norway?

The Conqueror

IN ENGLAND THE DANES, against whom Alfred the Great had fought so hard, finally gained enough power to rule that land for a few years. Then an Anglo-Saxon, Edward the Confessor, became ruler of England. Edward promised that when he died William, the Duke of Normandy, should become king. Normandy is the part of France about which you read in the last story— Normansland. But the English people did not wish to have William as their king. They chose instead an Englishman, Earl Harold, to rule over them. William did not like this choice. In the year 1066 he sailed to England with an army and began to fight for his right to be king. Although the English fought well, they were conquered by the Normans in a great battle at Hastings. William became King of England and was known as William the Conqueror.

The next story tells you about life in Normandy under the rule of William the Conqueror, who ruled there and in England at the same time. The way in which the people of France lived then was called feudalism. The king owned all the land, but could give it to his lords, or nobles. The lords were the kings vassals. Each noble to whom the king gave land had to agree to fight for his king. Each noble, in turn, required his tenants, the working people, to cultivate his land for him. From this land the workers had also to make their own living. Each tenant had a few acres of land to plant and harvest. Sometimes the tenants paid money to their lord instead of working for him. On each feudal estate there was a castle, or manor, where the lord lived with his family and his servants. There were also barns, a church, workshops, and the huts where tenants lived.

The next story tells about two girls who went to school together in the days of William the Conqueror. The embroidery on which they worked is still kept in France today, and is known as the Bayeux[1] Tapestry. In the Encyclopaedia Britannica you can see pictures of this embroidery. It is a famous work of art, and has been called "one of the noblest monuments of our history."

Silver Penny of William the Conqueror

With a jingle of bits and spurs, a rattle and creak of armor, the little procession drew to a halt at the top of the hill. "There, you can see the tower of the abbey church just above those trees," said the tall warrior who led the party. Alix, his twelve-year-old daughter, urged her small horse close

1. Pronounced *Bayoo*.

to that of her father. She pushed back the hood of her red woolen cloak from her brown curls so that she could see in the direction of his pointing finger. A square tower, crowned by a small, slender spire, rose above the yellowing autumn leaves that almost hid the rest of the convent buildings.

So their journey was nearly at an end! Alix tried to swallow, but there still remained a lump in her throat. At the end of this journey lay a parting! Within the shelter of those convent walls, she, Alix, was to remain in the care of the Lady Abbess while her father, the knight Bernard de Lacy and her brother, Gilbert, rode on to the Norman seacoast of France. There they were to take a ship for the strange, far land of England!

William, the first Norman King of England, was also Duke and ruler of their Normandy. To him Bernard and his son owed their service as knights whenever he should call them. Some of the Saxon earls of England had now revolted against the Norman King who had conquered them only ten years before. Alix knew this, and understood also that her father and brother had no choice but to obey the summons of their Duke, to whom both had sworn faith as vassals, or loyal subjects. Alix knew, too, that this adventure in England might mean the beginning of great fortune to her strong, handsome brother. King William had been generous in giving baronies and manors in England to knights who served him well. But she was thinking of herself—it was little to *her* taste to remain shut up by convent walls after the happy, free life she had led in her father's castle! Too free for a well-born maiden, her old nurse had often said.

Reaching the gate of the convent, they knocked; their knock was answered by an aged, black-robed sister who bade them enter. While the servants unloaded Alix's chests from the pack horses, Alix, together with her father and brother, followed their guide. The nun led them through a long, arched passage, across a courtyard where a few late flowers blossomed around a little sparkling fountain, along a shadowed cloister, and at last into the Abbess's hall.

The Abbess received her visitors graciously. A very great lady indeed was the Abbess of this convent. Under her rule were, by feudal law, many broad and fertile acres. Her tenant vassals included not only peasants and farmers, but knights and barons as well. Her black robe was of the softest wool, her linen fine and snow-white. Because this autumn day was cool, she wore also a cloak lined with rich brown martin—a fur which only those of noble rank were allowed to wear. She was not young, but she had an erect, commanding carriage. Her eyes were kind as she looked at Alix, who stood between the two tall, knightly figures.

Bernard de Lacy stated his errand. "And so our summons gives us no time to linger. We must be aboard ship before nightfall," he concluded. "It is with a heart thankful for your courtesy that I place my daughter in your care. A motherless maid of twelve cannot be left in a castle with only women servants, rough knights, and soldiers, no matter how loyal they are. Moreover, I know that here with you she will learn the gentle ways that befit her birth. She is nearly of an age to marry, and I see now that I have sadly neglected her training. But I love her well, and could not bear to send her away from me before this."

"I will care for her gladly, Bernard de Lacy," said the Abbess. "Already I have almost a score of young maids here in my school, not only from Normandy, but from other lands as well. Some, it is true, are novices planning to take our vows and remain with us as nuns, but others are here only for schooling and protection." She clapped her hands sharply together and a maidservant entered. "Send Edith here to me," said the Abbess.

When the messenger had disappeared, the Lady Abbess continued. "Each of our small dormitory rooms is shared by two girls. You, Alix, I shall put in with Edith, a ward of Duke William himself, who came to us only a week ago. She is a little older than you, but a sweet child. She will help you learn our customs and your duties."

As she finished speaking a light step sounded in the passage, and Alix turned to see a girl of fifteen or sixteen years standing in the open doorway. She was dressed in a simple, flowing gown of dark-blue woolen fabric. A White linen veil covered her head, but did not hide the brightness of her long, fair hair. Alix thought that she had never seen so sweet and lovely a face. Gilbert, too, must have shared his sister's opinion, for the girl's blue eyes fell and her cheeks colored before the boldness of his admiring stare.

Nor did this stare escape the Abbess, for when she spoke there was a hint of sharpness in her voice. "Edith, this is Alix de Lacy, who has come to stay with us. Take her with you and show her to the dormitory, where she is to share your room." To Alix she said, "Child, it will be far easier for you to say your farewell briefly here and now than to watch your kinsmen ride away— since go they must!"

The time had come, then, to say good-by! Alix could not keep back her tears, as she held tightly to her father and brother and kissed them as if for the last time. Then, with a long look at their dear, sorrowful faces, she let herself be led away.

The weeks and months that followed were strange to Alix. Everything here was so different from the life in her father's castle. There the days had been full of noise and bustle, of constant comings and goings. From dawn to dark she had heard the rough voices and loud laughter of the knights and men-at-arms, the clatter of horses' hoofs over the cobblestones and pavements of the courtyard that surrounded the high, square tower, or keep, that was her father's fortress and her home. All day the air had echoed with the sounds from all the workshops where the castle folk went about their tasks. Of late the chief sounds had been the clang and ring of the armorer's hammer as he worked upon the weapons and the suits of mail for Bernard and his son. Those suits of mail, leather shirts covered with overlapping metal plates, were the reason for the name "shining fish" that was given to the Norman knights by their enemies.

Then at night there had been the supper in the great hall of the keep. This great hall filled the whole of the space just under Alix's own apartments. Alix had sat proudly at the high table between her father and her brother to receive whatever guests had stopped for shelter that night. Sometimes it was a peddler, who spread his pack before her; sometimes a wandering barefoot friar on a pilgrimage from the Holy Land; sometimes a troupe of jugglers to amuse the whole company with their tricks of juggling and acrobatics; sometimes—and this Alix liked best of all—it was a minstrel with his harp, who would sing for them and think himself well paid for his skill by a good meal of roast meat and bread and wine and a chance to sleep on the soft rushes before the huge, roaring fire.

Alix's greatest pleasure at home had been riding on her own small, swift horse and hunting with a falcon on her wrist in the company of Gilbert. And now Gilbert was somewhere across the stormy sea, perhaps in deadly peril, while she, Alix, was close-shut in by these high walls where everything was so hushed, so quiet! Sometimes the quiet, broken only by the constant sound of the convent bells, was almost more than Alix could bear!

If it had not been for Edith she felt that she never could have borne the lonely stillness of the convent. From the first night she had known that Edith was her friend. Through the long, dark hours the homesick and weeping Alix had felt her roommate's comforting arms around her. Nor was Edith merely kind and pretty and gentle. She had an odd merry wit that could set Alix to laughing in spite of herself. But, although they had become fast friends, a barrier remained between them that Alix could not pass. Edith would never speak of her own home, her friends, or her family.

Quiet though the convent was, there was no idleness here. From the first hours of dawn, when the girls were called into the chapel by the early bells, until nightfall, their time was filled. The Abbess neglected no part of the training of her young charges. "If you are to be worthy of the station to which Heaven has called you, you must know how to oversee every task that you set for maid or man servant," she told them. "And how can you judge if a task be well done, unless you have done it yourself?"

So it was spin and weave, sew and mend, bake and brew from morning until night. Moreover, the Abbess had great skill in the nursing of the sick and wounded and in the use of healing herbs and medicines. This she taught to the girls, and also, to Alix's dismay, reading and the use of numbers. "You will often be left to rule in your husband's place when he rides away to war. You must at least learn how to read the rent-rolls, lest he find you but a poor steward of his property!" she said.

Of all the tasks, the one Alix liked the best was that of embroidery. The whole convent had long been busy on a great work—the stitching of figures of men and horses, castles and churches, in bright-colored wools upon a long, seemingly endless strip of linen cloth. When she had first seen the color and beauty of the workmanship, Alix had begged to have a part in it. But it was not until almost spring, when the Abbess was satisfied that Alix's stitches were skillful and fine, that she was allowed to sit at the embroidery frame in the high-windowed upper chamber where the work was being done.

"It is a great glory for the convent that we are allowed to do this," one of the girls told her. "No less a person than the Lord Bishop of Bayeux, brother to King William, has had it designed. It must be finished before the Bishop's new cathedral is dedicated, because on that day it is to be hung all round the nave[1] as a decoration."

"Do these figures tell some tale?" asked Alix as she pushed her needle in and out through the heavy linen.

Sister Cecile, the nun in charge of the task, looked up with surprise in her mild eyes. "You do not know? Then listen, for surely you will work better if you understand what it is that your fingers are fashioning," she said. She stood up and unrolled the finished end of the long band, so that Alix could see the very beginning of it. "Look," said Sister Cecile. "I will tell you the story as the embroidery pictures it. See the crowned and seated figure in this very first section? That is Edward, King of England, who, because of his piety, is called Edward the Confessor. He is speaking to one of his courtiers, who is none other than Harold, Godwin's son, who tried to keep our Lord Duke William out of his rightful inheritance of the crown of England!"

"Oh!" cried Alix, her face alight. "Then it *does* tell a story. Please go on!" She leaned eagerly over the

1. The central section of a cathedral.

next section of the work. The other girls also left their stitching and gathered around. All but Edith. She sat, her head bent low above the embroidery frame before her, her fingers moving just as before. "Go on, please, Sister Cecile," repeated Alix.

"Yes, my child. Here you see, next, Earl Harold starting on the errand that the King has sent him. He prays for a prosperous voyage. Then he crosses the sea. A storm rises, as you can see here, and the boats are blown ashore on the coast of Ponthieu[1] in Picardy instead of Normandy where Harold was going. Now here comes the Count Guy of Ponthieu, who discourteously makes the shipwrecked man a prisoner and takes him and his followers to his castle. Then our noble Duke William enters the story. He sends to the count to demand the release of the Saxon earl. Only after the sternest threats will the Count do this, but at last Harold is sent to our Duke in his castle at Eu.[2]

"Now you see by this picture with what friendship and honor the English earl is received by William. He is a guest at the Palace in Rouen.[3] When the Duke has to go forth to war against the Duke of Brittany, Harold, out of friendship, goes with him to fight by his side.

"In this group of pictures that follow, you can see the victories that they won together against the Bretons. There, too, you see how Harold was knighted by Duke William's own hand. Look well upon that picture, and upon the next one also! For here is shown the

1. The *eu* is pronounced like the *e* in *her*.
2. Pronounced *You*.
3. Pronounced *Roo-ahn*.

71

castle at Bayeux, with Duke William seated upon his throne with his sword in his hand, in full ceremony. And there is the figure of Earl Harold, standing between those two chests, a hand laid on each. He is swearing upon the most sacred of holy relics that he is Duke Williams liege man, and that he will help our Duke to win the English throne when King Edward shall have passed away.

"Now on again to Harold, returning to England laden with costly gifts. He is received by the aged King, who soon thereafter passes on to his reward and is buried with his fathers in Westminster Church. But when the royal crown of England is offered to Harold by the Saxon nobles, as is shown there, does he remember his sacred oath? No, for in the next picture you see him throned and crowned, while the people and nobles do him honor! But look! Heaven is not blind to his broken promise! See the great comet blazing through the sky, warning the people that evil will follow!

"Word of Harold's falseness comes to Duke William. At once he orders a fleet to be built and summons his vassals with their fighting men. Here you can see the carpenters at work felling the trees, and then the building and loading of the ships. Across the Channel sails the fleet, to land at Pevensey on the English shore. You can see how difficult it was to land the horses from the boats!

"Then, after a feast of thanksgiving for their safe voyage, the Normans must prepare for battle with the army of Harold. How hard and how long they fought, there at Hastings, is pictured plainly, as you can see.

Many brave knights and soldiers fell that day! Nor was Harold, false and forsworn though he was, without courage! With his brothers about him he stood fighting stubbornly. There he lies among his men at the last. Not until their king was killed did the Saxon English finally take to flight, and only then was the day won for the Duke.

"You see, the last part where we are working now is only done in outline. There is still much more work before it will match the rest. But I am sure that our Duke and King will be pleased when he sees it hanging there in the Cathedral of Bayeux. When summer is here again, he will return from England with his noble lady, Queen Mathilde, for the dedication."

"The King and Queen are coming to see it?" Alix's cheeks glowed, and she turned to speak with Edith. But Edith was no longer in her seat, nor was she anywhere to be seen in the sewing chamber. Alix looked about her, puzzled.

Then Claire, the girl who sat at the other side of Alix, nudged her. "Edith went out during Sister Cecile's story—and no wonder!" she murmured.

"But why?" asked Alix, wide-eyed.

"Don't you know? The Abbess has forbidden us to speak of it, but *everyone* knows!" Claire leaned closer to Alix over the embroidery frame as she whispered. "Edith is a Saxon—didn't you ever guess? Her father is a great earl in England. He never followed Harold, but because he is Harold's kinsman, King William mistrusts him. And, therefore, King William keeps Edith here as a pledge that her father will remain loyal to him.""

"Oh, I never dreamed..." gasped Alix, her face filled with pain. Suddenly she sprang to her feet, upsetting the stool under her. Without asking leave of the startled Sister Cecile she ran out of the sewing chamber, down the winding stone stairs, and out into the convent garden. Patches of snow still lingered where the shadows lay deepest. She must find Edith, tell her how sorry she was to have hurt her without knowing it!

Alix thought that she knew where to find her friend. Sure enough, there she was, huddled on a bench where the low, sweeping boughs of an evergreen tree hid a far corner of the convent garden. She looked up when she heard Alix's feet on the gravel path. Alix had planned the words that she would say, but when she saw the tears in Edith's blue eyes she forgot everything else. "Edith!" she cried, dropping down to the bench beside her. "I am sorry if I have hurt you. Why—why didn't you tell me?"

"Your father and brother were fighting my people," said Edith. "And I did so want your friendship! I was afraid that if you knew who I was you could not be my friend—and yet, truly, Alix, it has nothing to do with us."

"Nor has it changed me to know it!" cried Alix hotly. "I can never be an enemy to you, Edith. No matter where we go when we leave this convent, nothing can change us! Promise!"

"I promise!" said Edith. For a moment they sat there, close together on the bench and stared straight before them as though trying to see into the future.

Alix's cheeks were red and her lips set with determination. But Edith was older, and she had seen some of the darkness and cruelty of the world that lay outside these sheltering walls. She rose to her feet, shivering a little. "Come, it grows cold, and Sister Cecile will be calling us," she said.

Spring came and went. Now it was summer, and the garden was full of flower scents and bright colors. In the high-ceilinged sewing chamber the Sisters and their pupils worked without pause on the great embroidery that must soon be finished. Then one day the Lady Abbess summoned her charges into her hall, and told them that a great honor would be bestowed upon the convent. "The gracious lady, Queen Mathilde, wife of King William, is coming here to see our work," she said. "A messenger brought me word to expect her here tomorrow."

The girls were dismissed, but as they left the hall Alix heard the Abbess call Edith's name. "Wait here— I wish to speak to you alone," she said.

When Edith came out of the Abbess's door a few moments later, her face was so white that Alix was frightened. "What is the matter?" she asked.

"The Abbess has had a letter from King William," Edith said in a voice so low that Alix could barely hear her. "I must prepare to go back to England at once."

"Go away?" cried Alix in dismay. Then, putting all the brightness that she could into her voice, she went on, "Oh , Edith I'm sorry, but if it is to see your father again..."

"It is not to my father that I am being sent," said Edith, her face hard and cold as marble. "King William is giving me in marriage to one of his Norman knights—he does not even deign to tell me his name! As a prize—to a Norman!" She turned on Alix, her eyes blazing. "I will not do it! I will not marry a Norman! Oh, if they were all like you, Alix—it would be different! But this—! I tell you I *will* not! I will sooner die!"

"No—no!" Alix put her hand fearfully over Edith's mouth. "Don't say such words! Surely the King will not command it if he knows how you feel."

"He has already given too many nobly born Saxon girls as prizes for me to hope for any mercy," said Edith. "The King is a hard, cruel man, as even you must know!"

"But the Queen!" cried Alix, a hope dawning suddenly in her mind. "Queen Mathilde is gentle and kind. And she is coming here tomorrow! They say that she alone in all the world can move the King's heart. Speak to her, ask her to aid you! I know she will do it if she can!"

Neither Alix nor Edith slept that night. What would the next day bring? And long before sunrise the convent was astir with preparations for the Queen's visit. If only Mathilde were true to her reputation for kindness and piety, thought Alix! As a last resort Edith could take religious vows—remain here at the convent as a nun. Surely the Queen would not refuse that!

At last the great hour came! Followed by a train of knights and courtiers, Queen Mathilde rode up to the gates of the convent in a cushioned and curtained litter, or couch, carried between sturdy horses. "Her face is kind!" thought Alix, as the Queen passed between the rows of girls who bent low to the ground as she swept by. She kept Edith's slim, cold hand clasped tightly in her small warm one as they waited for the time when they dared to ask for an audience with the Queen. And then, surprisingly, Sister Cecile came through the throng straight toward them. "You are summoned into the Abbess's hall Alix, and Edith both!" she said, a little breathless with her hurrying.

Edith and Alix stared into each other's startled faces. The Queen was summoning *them*? Had she learned, somehow, of what they were planning to ask her? But how? Too puzzled to speak, they followed Sister Cecile and knelt, side by side, before the great chair where the Queen sat in state. Neither girl dared to raise her eyes until the kind voice spoke to them.

"So this is the fair Saxon!" said the Queen. "It is no wonder to me now that a young knight prefers her hand to a rich barony!" she said, and smiled upon both of the girls. The queen was a pleasant-faced, motherly woman for all her costly robes and jeweled coronet. "And you, Alix. You, too, are to return with me to England, for your brother wishes you also to be present at his marriage."

"My brother!" Alix stared up at the Queen, her eyes round.

"Why, of course—your brother, the young knight Gilbert de Lacy. So brave and so strong has he been that my husband, the King, offered him his choice of many broad manors. Instead, he asked for the King's ward, the lovely Edith here, whom he had seen for only a brief moment the day he and your father brought you here! The King has granted his wish, and Edith's noble father is pleased with the match as well."

The color was returning in a bright, lovely flood to Edith's white face, but still she was unable to speak.

"Then you will be my sister!" cried Alix, with shining eyes.

Queen Mathilde turned to the Abbess. "And so it goes," she said. "In your great embroidery there should be another section, to show the other form of conquest that has been taking place in England during these years since the Battle of Hastings. Though I think that our gallant young Gilbert is first to be conquered by a Saxon before he so much as set foot upon English land!"

The Great Journey

MANY OF THE PEOPLE who lived in Europe during the Middle Ages, from about 400 to about 1400, were good Christians. Led by the Church, of which the Pope was head, these people did many things to show how devoutly they worshipped God. One of the important ways to worship was to make a pilgrimage, or journey, to some holy place. The most important pilgrimage a person could make was to the Holy Sepulcher in Jerusalem. Here, according to the teachings of the Bible, Jesus was buried and from this sepulcher he rose on the day which we now celebrate as Easter.

For many years the people who ruled in Jerusalem were Arabs. Although they were not Christians, they did not keep the pilgrims from coming to their city. After a time the land in which Jerusalem lay was conquered by a different people, the Turks. These Turks hated Christians and did not want them to come into their country. Of course the Christians of Europe did not believe that the Turks should stop them from making pilgrimages to the Holy Land.

In the next story you will read about one of the greatest pilgrimages to Jerusalem the Christian people of Europe ever made—the First Crusade.

Darkness shut in about him; the air was stifling and hot. Denis ached in every muscle, but it was not his bruised and aching body that kept him awake that July night. A thousand thoughts followed close upon one another in his mind. Knighthood had come to him on this day that had just passed—knighthood, of which he had dreamed and for which he had worked for almost all of his nineteen years!

How long ago the first step upon this road seemed now, when he had been sent as a curly-headed, mischievous page to serve in the castle Chateldon! Then had come his term of squirehood when he left the castle to follow his master, the young knight, Josselin the Ruddy. And finally these last unbelievable years as arms-bearer—chief squire—to Josselin on the long march here to Jerusalem!

Yes, everything had been leading up to this hour of his knighthood. But very different had his knightship been from any that he had seen bestowed back there at home in the French province of Auvergne![1] Here had been no solemn ceremony, no night-long watch in the church, no buckling on of the golden spurs

1.Pronounced : *O-vern.*

80

and sword-belt. All such things seemed far away indeed. Between his home and Jerusalem lay countless miles of sea and land, and three long years!

Yes, it had been more than three years since he had ridden behind Josselin into the town of Clermont to hear what the Pope of Rome had come to tell his people.

Denis remembered that he had never seen such crowds! Following close behind his master, he had spurred his horse forward again and again to prevent the moving mass of people from separating them. Behind Denis the group of men-at-arms and archers followed as best they could on foot. All, at least, were going in the same direction—toward the western gate in the city wall of Clermont.

Josselin the Ruddy wore his full armor and rode his great war horse. Denis, too, wore his shirt of chain mail. But because he was yet only a squire, he could not wear the cone-shaped steel helmet nor carry the long, two-handed sword of a belted knight. Some day he would be a knight, he hoped devoutly, but he had not won that honor yet.

Denis's master had come on a peaceful errand into the town. The Pope's presence here at Clermont meant a truce in all fighting. But Josselin and his attendants rode armed, because between Josselin and his older brother, the Baron Raoul of Chateldon, there was a bitter hatred. A quarrel over the inheritance of their lands had arisen between them and of late it had grown fiercer. Denis knew that somewhere in this crowd Raoul and his men were riding too. Before nightfall the brothers would surely meet, and then the blood of one or both would be shed.

The crowd poured through the arched gateway below the belfry. Now there was room to move more freely. Like a gay carpet of throngs, in their bright holiday costumes, spread over the brown autumn fields. At last Denis could see the platform that was built in the open air high above the heads of the people. There the churchmen, in their robes of purple and crimson and gold, and the richly dressed nobles, waited for the Holy Father to appear.

Suddenly Denis saw his master's hands jerk so sharply upon his rein that his horse's head tossed upwards. Across the crowd he followed the young knight's gaze—yes, Raoul was there with his squire and his men, and armed too. Josselin's face flushed dark red as his eyes met those of his brother the Baron. Here in this throng they had to keep the peace, but their fierce looks crossed like swords. It would take more than a churchman's warning to keep them apart this day!

And then a sound of chanting rose in the air. The crowd moved and parted. Heads were bared and bowed as the people turned to watch the procession which approached through the city gate. In the midst of it, in a chair carried on willing shoulders, appeared Pope Urban, his golden vestments shining in the sun.

He ascended the steps of the platform and stood for all to see, a tall man with a thick, curling beard. Looking out over the upturned faces, he began to speak.

82

There was a stir and sudden pressing forward of the crowd. He was not speaking to them in Latin, but in their own French tongue, which the humblest of them could understand. How still the people were! They did not want to miss a word!

The deep, rich voice flowed out to them, and it seemed to Denis that it was reaching not only the ears of the people, but down into their hearts as well. For Pope Urban had come to Clermont with a message and a plea.

Far away across miles of sea and land, he told the listening crowd, a horde of heathens, called Turks, had swept down out of the plains of the East upon Palestine, the Holy Land. The beloved and sacred city of Jerusalem had been captured by them. Unlike the Arabs who had held Jerusalem before them, these newcomers would not permit other religions than their own to remain in the country. Moreover, they were unspeakably cruel; Christian pilgrims journeying to worship in the Holy City were captured and enslaved, tortured and slain without mercy.

This sad and terrible news had been sent to Pope Urban by the Emperor of Constantinople, who had seen his own lands overrun and many of his cities taken from him by these new enemies.

Whispers of horror swept through the crowd as the Pope told of the cruelty and wickedness of the Turks, the suffering of the Christians, and the dishonoring of the holy shrines by heathen hands. On and on went the Pope's deep voice. How could Heaven permit such deeds as he described?

From here and there in the throng came the sound of sobs as women wept; and the groans of men could be heard. Hardy squire though he was, Denis could feel hot tears in his own eyes. But he was not ashamed, for all about him peasants, townsmen, soldiers, knights as well with weathered, battle-scarred faces, bowed their heads to hide the sobs that shook them. All the sorrows of Christendom seemed to press down like an unbearable burden on all who heard the Holy Father's words.

Now the sound of the Pope's voice had changed. It rang like a trumpet call, stern and clear. Here in Christendom, he told them, on every hand men were fighting with other Christian men who should be their friends. Father fought against son, brother against brother! The Truce of God, which the Church had decreed in an effort to halt the senseless bloodshed, was being broken daily by men who called themselves knights, but who deserved not the noble name of knighthood. Let such men sheath their swords now, once and for all.

And then, the Pope cried, let men draw their swords forth again and pledge them to the noblest cause ever to challenge chivalry—the service of the Cross! Here, he said, was a war worthy of the Christian fighting men—a war to regain the Holy City of Jerusalem, the Holy Sepulcher itself! On such a journey they would ride at the summons of no earthly suzerain lord! The Lord of Heaven himself was calling them, and He would be their leader!

His voice ceased, and there came a stir, a murmur from the crowd like the sound of wind in forest trees. It grew louder, louder. The murmur changed to a vast shout that rose to the chill November sky. Swords flashed out, glittering as they swung. "God wills it!" cried the throng. "Dieu lo volt!"

Denis, shouting too, paused open-mouthed, for he saw an unbelievable thing happening. Through the crowd, scattering the people before him, Raoul of Chateldon was riding toward his brother. His sword was unsheathed, but it was in his left hand; he held it by the blade, with the crossed hilt above him. As he drew up beside Denis's master, he dropped the reins to his horse's neck and held out his hand.

"Josselin!" he said. "My brother! Will you take my hand? Will you ride with me on this great journey? For I know that I could find no braver comrade in all of this land of Auvergne!"

That had been the beginning. Thinking back, it seemed to Denis that a lifetime lay between that day and this hot, midsummer night!

Months of preparation had followed. The two young knights of Chateldon had set to their task seriously, for they were as shrewd as they were bold and fearless. They knew how long was the journey before them. Although they commanded but a small force of followers, they wished their men to be well provided with arms, gear, and provisions, and also with silver to buy food when it was needed along the way.

Such careful preparation was not made, Denis knew, by many of the other Crusaders. All that winter, through town and countryside, the word had passed like wildfire. There were strange tales, spread by rumor or by wandering barefoot friars: tales of the great "Journey of God," of the forgiveness of sins, the riches and rewards and plunder and glory that lay in the Holy Land, waiting for any who might go there!

Denis had seen crowds of peasants, townsmen, monks, even women and children, leave their homes to walk, ragged and barefoot, in the train of such leaders as Peter the Hermit and Walter the penniless knight. What had become of them in the years since then, Denis wondered. He had heard wild stories and had seen traces of their passing along the way to Jerusalem. But of all those pitiful, ignorant thousands, few indeed had lived to reach Constantinople, to say nothing of Jerusalem!

At last the two brothers announced that all was ready. From the tall keep[1] of Chateldon, through the surrounding wall of timber and stone, across the drawbridge into the village had ridden Baron Raoul, his brother Josselin the Ruddy, and their men. From the tower behind them Raoul's young wife had waved her proud and tearful farewell. On the shoulders of each knight, squire, man-at-arms, archer, armorer, even horseboy, who rode or walked out upon this great journey, was displayed the red Crusader's cross. And in each heart was carried also a vow each had made to

1. Keep: central tower of the castle.

86

win back the Holy Sepulcher from the heathen Turks no matter what the cost!

There had been days of prayer and fasting before the journey was begun. The priests had blessed their banners and swords and had given them absolution[1] from all past sins. The people threw flowers in their path as they rode. Denis followed his master, and behind Baron Raoul rode Stephen, his squire, a stalwart lad of Denis's own age.

How gay the journey had been at first! Many were the famous towns and castles that Denis had seen as they crossed Southern France and entered Italy. At Venice—the strange, lovely city rising out of the sea—the two young knights had met with the might noblemen, Count Raymond of Toulouse, and decided to take the same route as he to Constantinople. He was a wise old leader who had fought already against the Moslems[2] in Spain. Now he led a great army of vassals on this great adventure.

From some of Raymond's men Denis and Stephen learned that other armies were gathering too, led by the proudest lords in Europe. There was Godfrey of Bouillon, Duke of Lorraine, with his two brothers Baldwin and Eustace. There was also the brother of the King of France, Prince Hugh of Vermandois, and Stephen, Count of Blois. The Flemish Duke, Baldwin of Hainault, and Robert, Duke of Normandy, both led armies of knights and barons. And from Southern Italy and Sicily two mighty Norman warriors, Bohemund of

1. Forgiveness.
2. Those who believed in a religion known as Mohammedanism.

Taranto and Tancred, his nephew, were sailing soon. Six tremendous masses of fighting men, and with them as many more pilgrims and camp followers of all kinds, were on the march to the Holy Land!

Leaving Venice, the Count Raymond and the two knights set out eastward into the country of the Sclavs. And then, with winter rushing down on them, these Crusaders led by Count Raymond had found themselves in a wild mountainous land. Here, moreover, the people were hostile and many of the unarmed pilgrims who marched with the army were ambushed and slain by mountain brigands. Only by the most stubborn bravery did the Count of Toulouse and those who followed him win their way through the savage land.

Nor was that the worst trouble. Whether because of treachery or because of some error, Denis never knew, the Crusaders next found themselves attacked by bands of warriors under the banners of the Emperor of Constantinople—the very ruler whom they had come to aid!

But at last they reached the vast, imperial city of Constantinople that spread its marble palaces and domed churches along the waters of the Golden Horn.[1] There they could rest at last and gather provisions, and mend their armor. Whenever their work allowed, Denis and Stephen lost no chance to wander through the city and to marvel at the richness and luxury that they saw.

In Constantinople the two young knights of Chateldon had decided to join the famous champion, Tan-

1. The inlet which forms the harbor at Constantinople.

cred. Under his banner they enrolled with their followers, for, like them, he was young, valiant, and keen for battle.

Winter passed slowly. When spring had come they set forth. Six day's journey out of Constantinople lay the rich city of Nicaea, now held by the Turks. And there, in mid-May, the Crusaders had their first taste of battle with their Turkish enemies.

Denis remembered well his wonder and awe at the first sight of the walls of Nicaea![1] They had been built by the Romans, so men said. Looking up at them, yellow in the spring sunshine, Denis and Stephen wondered how mortal men could hope to take such a fortress! Walls they had seen before, in their own country —walls of earth and wood, even of stone. But these were higher and thicker than any they had ever known before! And a hundred towers were built along their length to give added protection to the defenders of the city.

But by siege, by violent attacks, and by well-planned strategy Nicaea was taken at last. The Crusaders' army moved once more on the road toward Jerusalem. They had felt eager and confident then, Denis remembered. The Turks who had tried to relieve the garrison in Nicaea had been beaten off with little trouble. Surely, nothing could stand against the power of the Christians' cause! Their supply wagons were loaded with food and spoils from the city of Nicaea. Denis and Stephen had sung together as they rode, proud to think that they were followers of the

1. Pronounced: *Nyceea*

great knight Tancred, who had proved himself the mightiest of all the Christian champions.

Then had come the battle of Doryleum. No easy conquest, this! The Turks had learned at last the power of the Crusaders and had gathered a great army under a leader who was called the Red Lion. Denis still remembered the horror and confusion in the Christian army when wave upon wave of the Turkish bowmen, galloping past on their swift Arab horses, had sent arrows into the ranks of the armored knights. The Turks themselves had kept out of the reach of the long swords and lances of the enemies. For a time it had seemed as though the Moslems would be able to celebrate a victory! Denis and Stephen, though they were only squires, had fought too on that day. Yes, and even pilgrims had caught up weapons that wounded men let fall and had defended themselves valiantly. At last the Christians won, and the great host moved forward again.

But now their road lay through a different land. The Moslems, in retreat, had laid the country waste. There was no food left anywhere; nor, on this high, hot plain, was there water to be found. It was a nightmare of suffering through which the Crusaders struggled slowly. Many of the horses died of thirst, and many knights had to walk in their heavy mail among the gaunt, hungry rabble of pilgrims.

Over a high mountain barrier the great host climbed wearily. There on the other side fortune blessed them, for they found a friendly folk, Armenian Christians, who gave them food and shelter. Without their guidance it would have been impossible to cross the last of the difficult mountain heights that lay before them. Once over these passes, the way was easier. Below lay a fertile plain, where the great city of Antioch waited beside a blue lake for its Christian deliverers.

After their long, starved march, it was no wonder that the Crusaders were greedy for the food that they found in the country around Antioch. But Antioch's walls were stout, her garrison strong. It would have to be conquered by a siege, if at all, the leaders decided. And now November had come, and with it came the winter rains that flooded the river and changed the country roundabout Antioch into a marsh. Winter brought cold, and hunger also, for the marchers had used up all the food they had found when they first arrived. Now they suffered for it bitterly.

Happily, however, a scouting party riding to the port of St. Simeon found many ships of England, Italy, and Byzantium[1] lying at anchor and loaded with supplies for the Crusaders. With new courage and energy they continued the siege of Antioch. And at last, after half a year, that city fell into the hands of the Christians.

Such joy as the weary conquerors took in their victory was short-lived. No sooner was the Christian army within the city walls than they in turn were besieged. A vast force of Turkish warriors, under their greatest leader, Kerbogha, surrounded the city. They had come too late to relieve the Turkish defenders, so instead they camped outside the walls and, in turn, pro-

1. Constantinople

ceeded to starve the Christians.

Side by side in the city the two dread perils of hunger and disease weakened the Crusaders day by day. And then, when all hope seemed lost, there came a miracle! A peasant boy had a vision of saints and angels who guided him to a spot where lay buried the Holy Lancepoint of the Crucifixion! With this sacred relic carried before them like a banner to give them strength and hope the Christian warriors marched boldly out of the city, and no infidel could stand against their attack! The Moslem army was crushed.

During the summer and fall that followed, the Crusaders rested in Antioch. There were many sick and wounded to be nursed back to health—among them Raoul of Chateldon—and there were dead to be buried. There was much work to do also. Armor had to be mended and new weapons forged. And, it was whispered, the great nobles who were the leaders of the Christian host quarreled constantly among themselves over the division of the riches found in the city. But of this Denis and Stephen knew little and cared less. So long as they could follow their gallant young masters and ride in the shadow of Tancred's crimson banner, such quarrelling meant nothing to them.

At last another year had begun, and the army was on the march again. Well mounted on fine Arab horses, the warriors rode southward through a long, smiling valley. The power of the Turks had been broken at last. Word of the might and courage of the Christian warriors had gone before them, and there was no resistance left in the Turkish infidels. Local chieftains of the Arabs gave them what they asked in food and supplies.

When pine-covered mountains rose to bar their path, the marchers turned westward to the seashore. They passed the ancient cities of Sidon and Tyre, the heights of Lebanon, and Acre. Soon after this, Denis remembered, a strange thing had happened. Stephen and he had been flying their falcons just as they had done at home in France. One hawk had overtaken a swift-flying pigeon and had struck it down almost at their feet. Picking it up, Denis had been surprised to find a small packet tied to its leg. Opening it, he found it to be a sheet of thin, parchment-like substance marked with writing. He had taken it to the Lord Tancred, who knowing Arabic, read the meaning of the message. It was a warning from one Moslem leader to another, telling of the Crusaders' advance. A message sent on the wings of a dove! Denis and Stephen talked long of this marvel.

And now as he lay in the darkness another memory came to Denis's mind. When they were only a few leagues from Jerusalem, Denis and Stephen had been wakened in the middle of the night by a summons. "Rise and make ready," they were told. Sleepily they had obeyed. A company of the younger knights, under Tancred, were arming, ready to ride. Where were they going at this hour?

It was to Bethlehem that they rode throughout that moonlit night, and, in the early dawn they entered the

Blessed City of the Nativity[1] itself! And there, over the Church of the Virgin, Tancred had placed his banner. He left a guard of knights to defend it, so the roving bands of Moslems, in retreat, should not defile the sacred place.

Then in the bright morning hours the young knights rejoined the host that was at last nearing its goal—the end of all their dreams and hopes—Jerusalem!

No matter how long he lived, Denis knew that he would never forget how the pilgrims, the soldiers, the knights, and the great lords sang together as they first came in sight of the gray walls and domes of Jerusalem. Many wept for joy, and all fell to their knees on the dusty earth to pray in that great hour!

Yes, Jerusalem was in sight, but the experienced warriors, looking up at those huge stone walls and mighty parapets, shook their heads. There was much to do yet before the city was theirs.

The slopes of the hills roundabout them had been stripped by the Moslems of all the timber that could be used in building ladders, scaling towers, or siege engines. How the infidels yelled and howled defiance as they stood on the walls of the city! But the Knights of the Cross had not come this far without learning much of the art of siege. They set to work without delay.

On the hills thirty miles away great trees were cut and from there carried with infinite toil to the city. At Jaffa, the seaport, lay a fleet of Italian ships from Genoa. Among the sailors were skilled carpenters and they

1. Birth of Jesus

94

came gladly to join in the task. Food was scarce, water scarcer, but nothing could stop the Crusaders now. Everyone, from the highest to the lowest, worked without rest. Nevertheless it was a full month and more before the leaders said all was ready for the attempt.

On the day of the attack the Moslems on the ramparts fought stubbornly. Again and again they threw stones, hot oil, and burning torches upon the scaling ladders and the siege towers which the Crusaders slowly pushed against the walls. All day the struggle continued, and when night came it seemed that the attackers had accomplished nothing, although many were slain and much of their careful building had been destroyed. But all that night they toiled to repair their work. When dawn came they set to battle again with undiminished bravery. And now Godfrey of Bouillon himself, who had been chosen as leader, mounted the highest of the movable towers. His closest kinsmen were behind him. Through the smoke and the flame that the frantic Moslems hurled into the wooden structure, Denis could see the steadfast figure of the great Duke as he waited for the moment when the drawbridge of the wooden tower should be let down. The Duke had sworn a vow that he would be the first to step foot upon the walls of Jerusalem!

Then Stephen had shouted to Denis through the noise and confusion. "Come!" he cried. "Our masters are ready. Tancred is forcing a gateway—we are to follow."

Of all that happened after that, of the battering

down of the gate, the entrance into the city, the wild battle that followed, Denis could remember little. He knew that in his hands he had held a long, two-handed sword and that he had swung it tirelessly. Stephen fought beside him, and their one thought was to keep in sight of the two young knights of Chateldon who seemed to have the strength of giants that day.

But he remembered well, when the city grew quiet at last, how they had followed their masters through the darkening streets, swords still unsheathed, until at last they found the Church of the Holy Sepulcher. Here they put up their swords. But then Josselin of Chateldon drew his blade forth again. "Denis!" he said. "You have fought well this day. Kneel down, that here in the door of this sacred place I may make you a knight as you truly deserve!"

Baron Raoul, not to be outdone, drew his sword also. Denis and Stephen bared their heads and knelt on the age-old gray stones of the street. Denis's heart beat as fast as though he were still in the thick of the battle. It beat so fast that he did not feel the stroke of the blade on his shoulder.

"Rise, Sir Knight," said Josselin. Denis stumbled to his feet, to meet not only the eyes of Stephen, his master, and the Baron, but those of mighty Tancred who stood leaning on his own red sword.

"Come," said the great champion. "We will wash from our hands this heathen blood that stains them, and then, all brother knights together, enter the Church of the Holy Sepulcher to give our humble thanks to Heaven for our victory."

All these things Denis remembered as he waited sleeplessly for the dawn to rise over the city of Jerusalem, rescued now at last from the hands of the infidels.

Twelve Bright Trumpets

IN THE LAST STORY you read about how a young squire became a knight because of his bravery during the siege of Jerusalem. The next story tells of what happened on a feudal estate in France when its young knights left it to take part in the Crusades.

Although there were many knights and barons who left their homes to ride off toward Jerusalem, there were many others who stayed at home; some of these took advantage of the fact that many manors were left without enough soldiers to protect them. Often they succeeded in stealing land, peasants, and castles from their rightful owners. Sometimes roving bands of thieves and homeless wanderers were easily persuaded to take part in such plundering.

In this story you will read how a girl held a castle from a robber baron until her brother returned from the Holy Land.

The Baron of Merveil[1] and his lady, dead of the same swift fever, had been but three days in their graves, when Arnulf of Mortain rode

1. Pronounced: *Mervay*.

up to the gates of the castle. In the great hall the young lady Rohais[1] received him. She looked like a tall child in her straight black gown. Her face was pale from much weeping, but her gaze was steady. At her side stood Simon, the captain of her men-at-arms, a gray-haired giant of a man.

His stiff words of sympathy spoken, Arnulf came bluntly to the point of his visit. "These be troubled times. I have come to offer the shelter of my castle to you, a young maid without protection. My lady joins me in this."

While he was speaking, the gray eyes of Rohais were upon him in courteous attention, but her thoughts flew past the burly, red-bearded figure. She knew well that Arnulf had been her father's enemy. He was a cruel, treacherous man, with a great ambition to gain more acres for his home, Mortain. She did not need Simon's warning growl in her ear to help her make an answer.

"I thank you for your courtesy," she told him. "But until my brother Fulke returns from the Holy Land, I must remain here as steward for his heritage. I do not lack protection."

"That she doesn't! Merveil is a stout-walled castle, and our lady has no lack of swordsmen and bowmen to defend it until our young lord Fulke's return," added Simon.

Arnulf scowled at the old man. "Until his return! But when will that be? Perhaps you had not heard, Lady Rohais, that a messenger has just lately brought

1. Pronounced *Rohay*.

sorrowful news? Our French knights have suffered grave disaster fighting under the walls of Jerusalem. Most of them were slain—the rest captured. That was months ago. You have had no word of your brother lately, I'll wager."

Rohais's face turned a shade paler. It was now as white as linen between the long bright braids of her hair. "No, we've had no word," she said. "But news comes slowly. I shall not believe he is a prisoner or dead until I know it to be true."

"Ill tidings are better faced squarely," said Arnulf, frowning. "Well, I'll leave you now, young Lady Rohais. I've warned you, and my offer still holds. Think well before you refuse altogether. Our Lord Duke is gone on the Crusade. With so many roving bands of thieves about, Merveil and its valley make too tempting a morsel to be left untouched long!"

There was more than a hint of threat in the look he gave to Simon as he turned his broad back and left the hall, his spurs ringing on the flagged floor.

Old Simon glared defiance after Arnulf. But when he looked into Rohais's face, his brows were drawn with trouble. "Too tempting a morsel to be left untouched long! I know which will be the first rat to try a nibble! Well, to be forewarned is to be forearmed! But this Arnulf is a bold ruffian with a large following, and I wish my young lord were home!"

"Then you do not believe what he said of Fulke..." Rohais's face brightened.

"Never for a moment! Arnulf made up that tale out of whole cloth!" Rohais felt a false bravery in

Simon's confident words, but nevertheless they drove away some of the chill that had numbed her heart.

"Simon, word of my father's and mother's death and the danger here must be sent to my brother at once! The messenger must be honest, discreet, and loyal, and everything must be done to speed him on his way!" Rohais said as she almost pushed Simon from the hall.

When Simon had gone on her errand, Rohais left the hall, too, and climbed a narrow stair that wound up into the highest tower of the castle. Whenever her mind was troubled, here she could find refuge and comfort. Far below, the valley of Merveil lay like a shallow golden cup, filled with the bright-leaved orchards.

Winding down the road from her castle, she saw the troop of horsemen from Mortain with Arnulf at their head. The sun caught at the points of their lances and on their burnished helmets. Dust rose behind them as they trotted into the wide street of the village. As Rohais watched, a peasant ox-cart lumbered out from between two thatched cottages and moved directly into the path of Arnulf's horsemen. Nevertheless the men kept on their course. Then Rohais saw a lance point dip. The goaded oxen turned sharply and the cart overturned. Its load of apples spilled into the dust. The horsemen rode on, unheeding.

Rohais's hands clenched. Her father's peasants had prospered under his wise, just rule. Never would she let them come under such a master as Arnulf! Never! she vowed to herself, there on the windy tower. No matter how long Fulke was gone, she would stay here and guard these poor people who were giving her their work and their loyalty in return only for the chance to live and till the fields in peace.

But Fulke! It was almost three years now since he had ridden away to the Holy Land. Rohais was only a small girl of ten when he lifted her into his great arms that last morning to say good-by. She could look down now and see the very spot where they had stood, there in her own tiny walled garden close under the tower of the castle. "And what shall I send you from Palestine, little sister?" he had asked as he set her on her feet again. "Shall I send you pearls from the Soldan's[1] turban, or maybe a small black slave to wait upon you?"

"Oh, no, Fulke," she had answered seriously, for she was always a grave child. "What I should like would be seeds and bulbs and roots for my garden. Here in the shelter of the walls the sun shines so brightly throughout the winter, I think that even flowers from the hot land of Palestine could grow. And when I see them blooming I shall know that I am looking upon the same flowers as you, though we are so far apart!"

He had thrown back his yellow head and laughed. :"Seeds and roots and bulbs it shall be!" Then he had returned to the courtyard through the low archway, stooping as he passed through because he was so tall. Rohais had watched him mount his waiting war horse, had heard the sounding of the horns as the whole cavalcade started on its way. And then she had climbed the tower to watch until the last faint cloud of dust had settled on the road that led out of the valley.

1. Ruler of the Mohammedans.

Fulke had not forgotten his promise. Every year, by the various messengers who brought news to the Baron from his son, had come packets for Rohais herself. They were wrapped in strange, beautiful silks. Each spring her garden had blossomed more brilliantly—a wonder for all to see. But this year there had been no message, nothing. The garden looked faded now in the late afternoon shadows. Rohais herself felt suddenly chilly.

She walked slowly down the stairway of the tower as though a weight were settling upon her with each step that brought her nearer to the ground. At the foot of the tower, however, she straightened her shoulders. She had been a child when Fulke went away, but she was almost a woman grown now. If he did not come back this year, she repeated to herself, steadily, she would still hold Merveil in his name.

Barely a week later another visitor stood in her hall. This time it was Father Drogo, Abbot of Hauteville. He was a kind, good man, but timid. "It surely is wiser, my daughter," he told her, "either to accept such shelter as Arnulf offers, rough though it be, or else to come with me to the safety of the convent. Unhappy news comes in from all sides. The word of the disaster to our crusading warriors has led the greedy petty barons and hedge-knights[1] to try for more land. It is only the matter of a little time before the countryside will be filled with robbery and murder as in the old days before our barons established the laws."

1. Men who falsely claim knighthood.

"I shall keep Merveil for Fulke," she answered. "I thank you, Father Drogo, but my mind is settled."

He, too, rode away across the valley. As he rode, he looked back sadly at the broad, fertile acres behind him.

But when he had gone, much of Rohais's courage disappeared. What if her confidence in the loyalty of her soldiers were merely pride, after all? Of Simon's faith she had no doubt, but he was an old man and the task of defending Merveil was a difficult one. An old man and a young maid to defend a castle and hold a barony? And still no word from Fulke!

That night brought rain that was driven by the wind through the narrow shuttered windows and that hissed into the logs that blazed on every hearth. Rohais sat sewing with her maids before the fire in her own small turret room. A servant pushed the hanging aside and stood in the doorway. There's someone at the gate, my lady," he said, "a peasant—a charcoal burner from the forest beyond Mortain."

"Send him in at once," said Rohais as she wondered what one of Arnulf's serfs[1] could have to say to her.

Into the firelight came a rain-soaked, smoke-grimed figure. "You wished to speak to me?" she asked kindly. The maids drew back their skirts in disdain.

The fellow told his story. That morning he had come upon a wounded man, a traveler, lying in the bushes not far from the road through the forest. He

1. Servants of a knight or lord.

had evidently been attacked by robbers who had stripped him of everything of value and left him for dead. When the charcoal burner came to his aid he was far gone, but before he died he had pressed a bundle into his hand and had said, "Merveil—the Lady Rohais!" So urgently did he speak that the forester could not refuse him. In fear of his life lest Arnulf should learn of what he was doing, the charcoal burner had come under cover of darkness to bring her the message and the packet.

Rohais opened it with hands that shook. Under the soiled covering was a strip of bright Eastern silk, and out of that fell a cluster of small dark roots—twelve of them! No one in all the world but Fulke would have sent such things to her!

"Tell me of this traveler—what did he look like?" she demanded, her heart pounding against her ribs.

The peasant wrinkled his brows in an effort to remember. "A bearded man with a flattened nose and a scar from ear to chin," he gestured with his finger.

Rohais pressed her hand against her mouth. "Giles—Fulke's servant! Oh, poor Giles!"

The charcoal burner was rewarded and sent upon his way. No need to warn him to keep his errand a secret!

Rohais's tears fell upon the roots. Poor, loyal Giles, to have died so near his home, after braving such miles of danger! But at least he had fulfilled his mission! She had these tokens that Fulke had sent her—at last she had word of him!

The next morning, after she had breathed a prayer

for the faithful Giles and another for Fulke, Rohais planted the bulbs in a row beside the wall of her garden. There the sun came first in the morning. Old Simon appeared through the gray archway as she patted the earth above the last of them. He, too, had been cheered by the wordless message contained in the packet. But now he looked down upon her with a frown bending his bushy brows.

Rohais stood up and brushed the earth from her palms. "What is it, Simon?" she asked.

"It was not robbers who slew Giles, but our neighbor Arnulf. Word comes to me that he grows bolder every day. If your brother Fulke could speak to you now, I think he would say to take shelter in the convent as the Abbot advised."

"And leave Merveil to Arnulf?"

"I and my men can hold it against him, without endangering you."

"And what of the peasants? Besides, if I were not here, do you think the men-at-arms would keep courage and stand against him for long?"

Simon dropped his honest eyes before her gaze. "Let that be as it might—you would be safe," he answered.

Rohais laid her hand on his arm. "We'll hold it together, you and I," she said. "I know that Fulke will return as soon as my messenger reaches him. But keep watch well!"

Peace seemed to fall over the countryside with the first snow of winter, but old Simon never relaxed his guard of the castle. With the spring thaws the news grew more alarming. "Arnulf's gathering all the rascals in the province about him!" Simon growled.

And then one day a man came riding down the valley, his horse in a lather of foam. "Arnulf is marching on Merveil!" he cried.

Simon had laid his plans well, and hardly had the news broken before the village sprang into activity. Oxcarts were loaded, flocks and herds were gathered together as the peasants hurried with all their movable goods inside the sheltering walls of the castle. They were barely in time, for over the edge of the valley a long, winding line of horsemen and foot soldiers showed dark against the melting snow. From the tower of the castle Rohais watched them come. They were a gang of ruffians gathered from everywhere and hungry for the plunder the smiling valley offered. Finding that the peasants had fled, they revenged themselves by setting fire to the thatched-roofed cottages. The flames burned long into the night.

The light of the burning cottages glowed on the red beard of Arnulf as he rode up to the closed gate of Merveil. His herald blew a long blast of his horn, and Rohais stood above the archway to hear what he had come to say.

"Open your gates, yield your castle, and I promise no harm to you or your people," Arnulf told her. On either side of him men held torches that streamed sparks into the wind. The faces that looked up at her were harsh and cruel, but the thought of Fulke gave her courage.

"The castle is not mine to yield. When my brother

Fulke returns, he and his fellow knights will give you your answer!" She tried to speak boldly, but the wind caught her words and carried her voice away—it sounded small and uncertain.

Arnulf grinned. "Always—'When my brother returns'! Your brother has not yet set foot upon these shores. There's ample time for all my work before his coming!"

"Surely you do not dream that I would take your word for that, Arnulf of Mortain!" her voice was clear and scornful.

"Maybe not my word, but what if I gave you Fulke's own?"

Rohais caught her breath and clutched at the parapet to steady herself. "Fulke's word? No, I do not believe you!"

"Listen, then—let me give you the news of your brother. I have here a message that was written to you, but by chance"—he repeated mockingly—"by chance it has come to my hands instead." He motioned to the herald at his side, who unrolled a strip of parchment.

Close at her elbow Simon muttered, "So he has waylaid another messenger!" But Rohais was leaning out over the wall while the herald held the parchment to the light of a wind-blown torch.

"To my sister Rohais. I have sent you twelve heralds, Moslem converts from the Holy Land. When you see them stand beside your tower wall, arrayed more brightly than Solomon, the King of Jerusalem, when they blow their trumpets, then look for me close behind them." The herald finished and rolled the scroll again, and Arnulf nodded. "So you see, my young lady, when I learned this I set my men to watch every road. Twelve brown Paynims[1] cannot enter this province unseen, and we shall have good warning of your brother's approach! We shall prepare a warm welcome, you may be sure! If you yield the castle, I will send you safely to the convent at Hauteville, and your brother and his friends may ride unharmed for all of me. It is only the castle and valley of Merveil that I want, No bloodshed, I promise you! But refuse, and your brother dies in ambush; the castle will fall at last to our siege, with mercy for none!"

But Rohais's face had grown radiant as the meaning of Fulke's message came to her. She leaned over the wall. "Thank you for the message!" she cried. Since I know that my brother is on his way, I shall wait for him!"

Still smiling, she watched the men withdraw from the walls to form their encampment surrounding the castle. The siege had begun.

"Well," old Simon asked her when morning came at last. "Those were brave words of yours last night, but what was the use of them? Do you wish your brother to walk into Arnulf's trap? And how long, think you, can we stand siege with so many people to feed?"

Rohais's eyes sparkled. She took Simon's hard, rough hand in hers and led him into her small wall-encircled garden. Here the snow had long been gone and leaves and buds were showing above the brown earth. "My brother's heralds are already within our

1. Mohammedans from Jerusalem.

walls!" she told him and pointed to a row of slender green stalks standing against the sunniest wall. "The twelve brown roots have grown, and I can see plainly that they are some sort of Eastern lily. Are not the lily blossoms shaped like trumpets? And what does the Holy Book say about their raiment—'not Solomon in all his glory'—O Simon, can we not stand any siege when we know that Fulke is truly on his way?"

And so it happened that by the time the last bright fragrant trumpet-cup had opened, the besiegers looked up one morning from their campfires to see the sun flashing on lance and helmet. The great banner, emblazoned with the Crusaders' Cross, strained stiff in the wind above Fulke and his company of knights as they rode over the rim of the valley! To stand and face untrained men-at-arms was one thing! To stand and face these armored veterans quite another! Arnulf and his rabble disappeared like snow under spring rain, and Merveil flung wide its gates to welcome its master home!

Echo Over Runnymede

WHEN KING RICHARD of England (Richard the Lion-Hearted) was captured by enemies on his return from the Holy Land, John of England tried to convince the people that Richard was dead. He himself wanted to become king! His plan did not succeed at that time, but later, when Richard died, John did become king. He was one of the most cruel and greedy kings England has ever had.

King John always needed money and did not care how he got it. For example, the feudal lords of England, in order to keep their lands, had to go to war whenever the King wanted them to. King John would call them to war and then would not let them return to their homes until they had paid him large sums of money. The King also took bribes, payments of money, for doing things he should not have done at all, and he taxed all his people heavily.

The barons of England knew that the English law of the land gave them certain rights. They also knew that King John was not obeying the law. They agreed to give John one more chance to respect their rights. But King John did only what pleased him, and to be a good and honest king was not pleasing to him. He cared nothing for the rights of the nobles.

Finally, in 1215 at a place called Runnymede, the

barons, the wealthy merchants of London, and the churchmen of England forced King John to sign a charter, called the Magna Carta. This charter was a written statement of certain things which King John could do and things he could not do. The charter was important because it said that the laws of England were stronger than the King and that if the King did not obey them, the nobles could force him to do so.

During the years since the Magna Carta was signed, it has become the symbol of the right of people to say how they should be governed. It meant, and still means to many English people, what the Declaration of Independence means to us today.

This story tells about a boy who lived in England when the Magna Carta was signed by King John.

With the spirited little horse prancing under him, with his best cloak of fine scarlet wool floating behind him, and the golden-hilted dagger that his father had given him that morning at his side, Geoffrey knew that never in all of his ten years had he been so proud or so happy! Of course, ever since he could remember, he had looked forward to this day. He had known that sometime he would leave his home to take service as a page in the household of one of his father's friends—knight or baron. But he had not dreamed of anything like this!

For Geoffrey was not going to the manor of anyone of his father's own rank. Rather, Geoffrey was on his way to the castle of his father's suzerain lord, the mighty Earl who had given Geoffrey's father the Manor of Orville and all its lands. Years had passed, it was true, since Sir William, Geoffrey's father, had followed the Earl on the Third Crusade to the Holy Land, led by King Richard the Lion-Hearted. The Earl, however, had not forgotten the brave service William had done him. And so as a reward he had sent one of his own squires, Amory, who now rode at Geoffrey's side, to bring the boy to his castle and begin his training.

As they reached a hilltop above the valley, Geoffrey turned in his saddle. He wanted a last look at his home, for he knew that it would be long before he saw it again.

From the hilltop the great stone tower, the high, pointed gables, and the out-buildings of his father's manor looked tiny in the distance. The morning sun glinted on the water of the moat that encircled the protecting walls of the manor house. As he watched, Geoffrey saw an ox-cart, driven by one of his father's serfs, lumber through the gate and over the drawbridge and then head toward the grain fields where peasants were already harvesting the ripe grain. The cart moved slowly along the dusty road and past the mill whose dripping wheel flashed with each turn. Beyond the thatch-roofed huts of the village stretched the cultivated land of the manor. The many narrow strips of land tilled by the various peasants ranged in color from ripe yellow, through green, to earth-brown. The brown strips meant that the fall plowing was already begun.

Having looked his fill, Geoffrey turned his face forward once more. If he felt a moment of regret at leaving his pleasant home, the thought of where he was going drove it instantly away. His blue eyes were shining as he met those of the gaily dressed young squire, Amory, who had paused, too, to look back. William of Orville's manor was not large, but it lay in a fertile, well-watered valley. He gave constant thought to the care of his acres; there was no knight in this part of England who had a better right than he to feel proud of his lands.

"It is a fair enough valley," said Amory. "But when you see it again, it will look small and mean to you after the Earl's great castle!"

Geoffrey flushed. "It will never seem mean to me!" he said hotly. "The Earl may have higher towers and broader lands, but no other place will ever be so dear to me as this!"

Amory laughed good-naturedly. "Stoutly spoken! And right words enough, because it is to learn how to hold this manor when it is yours that you are now starting on this journey."

Then they touched spurs to their horses and rode forward again through the green and gold of the late autumn countryside. Many miles lay between them and their goal. Behind them the men-at-arms and the servants with the pack animals talked of many things and joked together. But Geoffrey had only one thought in his mind. Question after question he asked of Amory, who answered them all as well as he could.

"Yes, the Earl has many squires," said Amory. "Three of them are now ready and waiting for knighthood. Perhaps we shall have another tourney[1] soon in their honor—you would like that, Geoffrey! Then there are more than a score of noble knights and barons who serve the Earl's household, besides several hundred fighting men of common rank. Archers, pikemen, axemen also. As for pages—I never stopped to count them!" He looked down at Geoffrey with a smile. "You will not lack for company!"

On and on they rode; morning passed into noon. When the sun was halfway down the western sky they entered a thick forest, and there, Amory told Geoffrey, the Earl's private lands began. "Here is where we often come to hunt," he said. And as they came out of the wood, he pointed to a river that cut through a smiling, level valley. "There beside the river, where the reeds grow, we fly our hawks and falcons. But look! Before you is the castle!"

At a sharp bend in the river and set on a high, rocky bluff stood the great mass of towers and battlements that marked the end of their journey. Geoffrey could not keep back a gasp of wonder and admiration. The light of the setting sun lay behind it and the castle seemed to rise to a stupendous height out of the golden, mirroring water! Over the topmost of the many towers floated a banner that showed crimson against the sky.

1. A tournament or competition of knights at which prizes were awarded to those who proved themselves the most skillful at mounted fighting with lances.

"Oh, to own a castle as noble as that!" cried Geoffrey. "The Earl must be the happiest man in all the world!"

"If riches and a great name mean happiness, you would be right," answered Amory, soberly for once. "But it is not so simple as that. An Earl who is a tenant-in-chief to the King has much to trouble his mind that men of fewer responsibilities know nothing of. Especially"—he drew his brows together in a scowl—"when we have such a king over us as John Lack-Land!"

Geoffrey had often heard his father speak bitterly of the greed and cruelty of King John, who had come to the English throne at the death of gallant Richard. The laws of the land meant nothing to this ruler! No one was too high, no one too humble, to escape his tyranny. From the poorest peasant, as well as from the rich and the great, he took anything that he could find, and imprisoned and killed whoever dared to oppose him.

But now at this moment Geoffrey could think of nothing but the castle that appeared ever larger before them as they rode nearer. Before they reached the first encircling wall of stone, they were halted at the outer barbican, or high fence of heavy timbers, that stretched across the point of land where the castle stood. A frowning, watchful face appeared above the gateway. "Well, Peter, do you not know us for friends?" asked Amory. The man's frown changed to a welcoming grin. The hinges creaked and the gate swung wide to admit them.

Inside the barbican was a flat, grassy meadow marked off by a number of low fences. As they rode forward toward the castle, Geoffrey saw a cloud of dust rising at one end of the field. A group of horsemen in full armor were galloping across the open space. Engaged in a sham battle, they were practicing their skill with blunted spears. These, then, were the "lists" of the castle, the fields where the tournaments of which he had heard so much took place!

Now they had reached the edge of the moat. Beyond rose the castle walls, sheer, frightening, and enormously high, flanked by jutting towers. The drawbridge lay across the moat. The portcullis[1] was raised, but the heavy, metal-studded oaken gates were closed. A porter recognized Amory at a glance, however, and a narrow side gate, wide enough for only one horseman at a time, was opened to admit them. Through this they passed in single file into a space within the first circle of the castle walls—the bailey of the castle.

As they dismounted and gave their animals to the care of waiting stable boys, Geoffrey glanced eagerly round him and thought that never had he seen so busy a place as this! It was like the farmyard of his manor at home, but with the noise and activity multiplied a hundred times. There were many wooden buildings lining the high stone walls—a long row of stalls for horses, a cow stable, dwellings for servants, a cook house, workshops and storehouses of every kind. A blacksmith shop with an open front stood at one end. The blacksmith was even now striking ringing blows on his anvil and sending out sparks at every stroke. Another man in a leather apron worked the bellows of the forge fire.

1. A frame of iron bars hung over the gateway of a castle and lowered to block the entrance.

At the far end stood a long shed whence came the shrill, harsh cries of falcons and hawks. In the center of the open space was a well where women were filling pails and pitchers and others were washing linen. Not far away stood a great bake oven. Dogs, pigs, and chickens were running everywhere under the feet of the busy servants and the idling men-at-arms.

These men greeted Amory with respect and stared at Geoffrey as the two passed between stone towers, through an open gateway, and under a heavy arch of stone to the inner court of the castle. Farmyard animals were not allowed here, it was plain to see. The flagged pavement was swept clean; the servants here were dressed in the Earl's rich livery. The towers and battlements that enclosed this space were even higher and thicker than those about the bailey.

In the center of the courtyard stood a small, beautifully built chapel with lacy spires and high-arched windows of colored glass. Geoffrey was staring open-mouthed at this when Amory pointed to a single huge and massive tower whose shadow lay darkly across the courtyard.

"That is the ancient keep, the tower built here by the first Norman baron," he said. "Most of the other walls and towers were built by our Earl's own father, who brought the design from the Holy Land. Our own master built the chapel in which to worship, and his private palais[1] where he lives. But the old tower is still our fortress—there we could make a brave last stand if

1. Pronounced *palay.*

King John should do as he has threatened and come against the Earl with his army."

"Lay siege to this castle!" cried Geoffrey in surprise and a little dismay. But Amory was already climbing the steps of another structure that was built in the same light and elegant way as the chapel, with high-arched windows and many chimneys. "This is the dwelling of our lord the Earl," said Amory. He opened the heavy door. The great hall is only newly completed. I'll wager you never saw anything like it before!"

And indeed Geoffrey never had. Wide-eyed he gazed about him—at the arched and painted roof, so high that it seemed lost in shadow; at the windows set with real glass, cleverly held in place by strips of lead; at the walls, hung with bright tapestries; the huge fireplace, the carved benches, and cushioned chairs. Long tables were being set by the servants in preparation for supper. They were covering them with linen cloths dyed in the gayest colors of scarlet and blue. Never had Geoffrey seen so many dishes of fine silver, even of gold. There at the end of the room was the high table, set on a platform above the rest and covered with a canopy of fringed and embroidered velvet; and there was the throne-like chair that was the Earl's high seat.

Geoffrey would have liked to linger here, but he knew that he must find the Earl and pay his homage. So he followed where Amory led the way toward a door that was guarded by a young squire. As they crossed the hall, the green rushes and sprigs of mint that had been freshly scattered on the floor gave out a spicy odor from under their feet. The guard opened the door and parted the curtains to let them pass. "This is the Earl's chamber," Armory whispered.

Though not so large as the great hall, the Earl's chamber seemed huge enough to Geoffrey. The first thing he saw was a group of people at the far end near the windows—a group of ladies dressed in silk as bright as butterflies. They were listening while a young man in rich clothing sang in a high, pleasant voice to the strumming of a lute. "That is the Countess—the lady dressed in blue!" murmured Amory. "And the singer is Messier Noel, the famous troubadour from France."

On the other side of the room stood a great bed. Its canopy almost touched the ceiling, and from its carved and painted frame hung curtains of embroidered velvet.

But Geoffrey had eyes now only for one thing— the circle of light shed by a tall wax candle set on a massive table. There, in a high-backed chair, sat a man listening while an aged clerk read aloud from a sheet of parchment. Even if he had not been seated in his chair of state, dressed in clothing of velvet and princely fur, Geoffrey could not have mistaken this man for anyone but the lord of the castle! No more could he have mistaken a royal falcon for a lesser bird! He followed Amory across the hall and knelt beside him at the Earl's footstool. And there he felt himself beginning to tremble and he wondered wildly if he could remember the speech which his father had taught him so carefully to speak at this moment!

But when a deep voice spoke to him, he looked up into a grave, strongly lined face that was nevertheless smiling at him kindly. Geoffrey forgot his panic and the words came. "My father, William of Orville, Knight, sends you his homage by me, Geoffrey, his youngest child and only son," he said, his voice strengthening as his courage returned. "And from this day forward I pledge you my service, my faith and my loyalty forever, in body and in heart."

"Welcome, Geoffrey, for your good father's sake," said the Earl, motioning the two boys to their feet. "I can see the likeness to my friend and comrade in your forehead and your chin, but I think that your blue eyes are from your fair mother. You will take your place among my young varlets[1] and learn all that a page and a squire must know. And when the time comes, if you have deserved well of me, I myself will make you a knight."

Then he turned to speak to the clerk who stood at his elbow. "Yes, that letter is now written as it should be. Let it be sealed. And you, Amory, go call a messenger to me—tell him to be ready to ride out tonight."

Amory hurried away. Geoffrey, standing aside, watched the clerk melt the sealing wax, drop it on the folded parchment and the cords that tied it, and stamp the seal with the great, carved ring which the Earl removed from his forefinger. Then, when the messenger appeared, the Earl handed the letter to him. "Take this to the Archbishop of Canterbury," he said. "Give it to him and to no other! Above all, let it not fall into hands friendly to King John!"

1. Knight's attendants—pages, squires, and so on.

The messenger bowed and was gone. Then the Earl turned again to Amory. "Show Geoffrey to the pages' quarters. And after this I charge you to keep a friendly eye upon him, for you remember, I know, how strange all this seems at first to a small lad away from his home for the first time!"

He dismissed the two boys with a wave of his hand and turned again to the waiting clerk. Geoffrey followed Amory out of the door to begin his new life here in the castle.

It was indeed all new and strange to Geoffrey. But he had had good training at home to prepare him for this time. From his father he had learned to ride, to hunt with hawks and with hounds, to carry and to use the light swords and spears that a boy of his size could handle. From his mother and older sisters he had learned the rules of courtesy at the table and in the great hall. And from his father's chaplain he had learned the beginnings of reading and writing. Thanks to this training, and to the kind interest of Amory, he soon found himself accepted as part of the castle household. His cheerfulness and good nature, as well as the fact that he was strong and well grown for his age, kept him from too much bullying at the hands of the older boys.

The great Earl, busy with so many duties, found time to give him little but an occasional glance and gracious word. The Countess, however, took him under her special care when she found that he had a clear, true voice and could play skillfully upon the lute. She was much younger than her noble husband. She was his second wife whom he had brought here to England from the sunny south of France. Provence had been her home, the land of sweet-singing troubadours. Her chamber was hung with the gayest of Eastern silks. Saracen[1] carpets covered the stone floors, and the room seemed always filled with songs and laughter. The Earl's older children were married and living on their own lands, but the Countess's tiny daughter was the darling of the castle. Geoffrey thought that only the Holy Mother and the Child themselves, pictured in the illuminated Book of the Hours,[2] were a lovelier sight than the young Countess and the little Lady Maris as they sat in the window seat with their golden heads close together and sang the gay songs of the Southern land!

But as the autumn drew on towards the winter, outside the Countess's bower there was little gaiety. During these months Geoffrey heard more of what Amory had said on that first day—that there was a fierce quarrel raging between King John and certain of his greatest barons, of whom the Earl was one. In November the castle folk watched their lord the Earl, with a company of knights and horsemen, ride out and away to Bury St. Edmund's the shrine of an ancient Saxon Saint. There he was to meet with other mighty nobles and swear a solemn oath that they would stand fast together against the tyranny of the King and so win back from him the ancient liberties and laws of England.

Even Geoffrey, the youngest page in the castle,

1. Mohammedan.
2. A prayer book, usually beautifully illustrated in color.

knew well what such resistance to a ruler might mean. King John was an enemy to be feared. He had heard tales of what happened to others who tried to go against his will. King John had few friends, it was true, but he had gold. With it he had bought the service of foreign soldiers who were skillful in war and siege-craft. Word flew about the country that he had sworn an oath himself, with a oath to crush any barons who dared to match power with him! Moreover, he had besieged and taken castles before this! The fate of the owners of those castles had been horrible, enough to make the blood run cold! No wonder the Earl's brow was wrinkled with care when he returned from the secret meeting, and that he set to work at once to bring in supplies and weapons to withstand any siege that King John might make.

Armorers toiled long hours, and knights, squires, men-at-arms, and archers practiced their warfare daily. The pages, crowding around the lists outside the castle, longed for the time when they could carry swords and lances also! The winter grew colder. Christmas came and passed, but there was little of the usual feasting and merry-making. In the evenings, round the great log fire in the hall, Geoffrey and the other pages gathered to listen to the tales of siege and battle told by two old veteran knights, Sir Eustace and Sir Malcolm.

The new year brought word that made Geoffrey's heart almost fail him. The earls and barons had told the King that unless he fulfilled before Eastertide the pledges that they had demanded of him, they would deny the loyalty they had sworn him as their king. Deny their loyalty and faith? Break their oaths to the king? How could they dare? The keeping of a feudal oath of loyalty seemed to Geoffrey the most sacred duty of man! But Geoffrey's trust in the Earl's honor was complete. If the Earl renounced the King, that was surely the right thing to do!

It was during the late winter that something happened to still at last the songs and laughter in the Countess's bower. A herald and two attendant knights, with a lordly train of followers under the banner of King John, arrived at the castle gate one snowy evening. Only the three leaders were admitted by the cautious warder of the gate, but these three marched boldly into the great hall wearing their full armor, their helmets, and their swords. The Earl received them with his wife and retainers about him. Geoffrey, standing behind the Countess's chair, wondered at their discourtesy in thus coming armed into the hall!

"We bring you commands from your master the King." said the herald in a loud, harsh voice. "He has heard that you are among those of his vassals who defy his rightful powers. If this is not true, then he demands a token from you to prove your loyalty, and so escape his wrathful punishment. You are hereby commanded to put your young daughter into his care, to be hostage for your good faith."

There was a sharp gasp from the Countess and a shout of rage from the Earl's followers. Swords leaped from their scabbards. The King's messengers drew together and looked about them fearfully. The Countess clasped her little girl to her, her face pale. All eyes were turned on the Earl.

His voice was calm and quiet when he spoke. "Tell King John that I refuse. Tell him that I am indeed one of those who have demanded king's justice from the King. Tell him that I would sooner trust my child to the care of my meanest serf than to that of a king who has so often broken his word! Take that message to your master. And also the warning that he has only until Easter Day to decide whether or no he is to remain the King of England!"

When the herald, the knights, and their company had ridden away again through the snow, the castle folk settled more grimly than ever to the task of making ready for whatever the King might do. There was no limit, as they well knew, to the cruel things he would do to them once he had the power.

But happily for them, time proved that King John had met his match at last. Try as he would, he could not change the fixed purpose of the barons to stand together against him. Now they were supported by the common folk as well. Nor could he wring from his exhausted, stubborn people enough gold to hire any more foreign troops to make war against nobles and common folk.

With the passing of Easter no word had come from King John. Then Each Earl, baron, and knight summoned his vassals and fighting men. A great army of them marched on the city of London where King John had taken refuge. Amory and Geoffrey, riding in the Earl's train, shared the joyful surprise of the army when the citizens of London, after only a brief time of talking together, flung open their gates and joined with the barons against the King! When he saw London itself turn from him, King John fled from the city to his castle at Windsor. Only a small number of courtiers and hired soldiers followed him there, but from Windsor he sent word forth that he was "graciously pleased to grant his subjects' prayers!"

"The barons know slippery John too well to disband their armies," Amory told Geoffrey. There in the peaceful June weather, in the countryside by the river Thames, they made a great camp. The leaders of the Church and State, with some of the worthy merchants from London, came together to make their plans. The place of the meeting was called Runnymede—a meadow, so it was said, where the ancient Saxons had often met in time long past to make their laws.

The King's word was not enough, they decided. The King must put his name and seal to his promises. It must be done solemnly, with ceremony, and before many witnesses. And the terms of this charter must be carefully and wisely drawn up. While the document, the Magna Carta, was being prepared, King John rode over every day from Windsor to Runnymede to try to make changes in it, but all in vain. He was as bold as he was cruel, thought Geoffrey, after seeing how few were the followers who rode behind the King through the scowling, angry crowds.

Old Andrew, the Earl's clerk who was employed in copying the charter, tried to explain to Geoffrey what it meant. Much of it was beyond the boy's understanding, but some of the old man's words stayed in his mind.

"It is pattered after the laws of Good Alfred and those of Edward the Confessor and also the charter given to the English people by Henry I," Andrew said. "But parts of it are new, for it is written to protect common men and villeins[1] against injustice, as well as those nobly born! In one place the King is to swear 'No man will I deprive of his freedom or his goods except by the lawful judgement of his peers[2] and the law of the land.' And in another, 'To no man will I sell, or delay, or deny justice.' "

"Those are good laws, surely," said Geoffrey. "But tell me, will King John keep such promises when once he has power again?"

"The barons have thought of that," answered Andrew. "They are forming a council of twenty-five of their number whose duty it will be to keep watch over the King in this matter."

At last the date was set for the signing of the document by King John. During the warm hours of the night before, Geoffrey, lying just outside the Earl's tent, could not sleep. When dawn came he was up with the sun. He had no duties for that day and he wanted to get a good place on the riverbank — a place where he could have a view across to the island where the ceremony was to take place. All the morning before he had watched carpenters build a great pavilion there. Now it stood ready, covered with the richest and gayest of cloth, while banners and pennants floated and snapped above it in the summer breeze.

1. Free peasants.
2. Equals.

Early though Geoffrey was, others were there as soon as he. Hordes of folk from town, village, and field came streaming along the river road and across the meadows. Such crowds he had never seen before. Boats, too, filled the river which here at Runnymede ran so swiftly. But space was left clear for the richly decorated barges that were to carry King John and the barons across the water to the island. Round-eyed, the people stared at the camp of the barons' men, at the barges, at the pavilion across the water. What was it all about, this quarrel between King and lords? Did it really concern them also, as some said? Was something being done that would ease the hard life of the poor folk? Or was it merely another of the wars between the great and powerful ones? There was an eagerness in their faces and voices as they moved about the sunny fields. If it had not been for a certain strained and anxious feeling in the air, it might have been a festival or a holiday.

But then the knights on their great war horses, followed by their squires and men-at-arms, began to approach the river from their camp. The crowd, parting before them like water, stared up into the stern faces under the helmets and knew then that this was no festival! This was grim and deadly earnest. These men rode in full armor, their long swords by their sides. Let the King bring on his French and Flemish troops if he dared, they seemed to say. They were ready for him!

All that bright, warm June morning the crowds waited. As the hours dragged on, rumors began to pass through the throng. What if the King had slipped away from Windsor? What if he had been playing them a trick all this while? He was crafty and cunning, he had done such things before. The people stirred about uneasily; the men-at-arms leaned on their spears; the knights in their heavy armor sat their restless horses, waiting, waiting.

And then someone gave a cry. Along the road that followed the river a cloud of dust was moving. Banners and pennants showed above the dust; below it, a company of horsemen. The King! The King had come at last!

Through a heavy silence far more expressive of the people's hatred than curses, the cavalcade came on and then stopped at the barge landing. Pressing close, Geoffrey saw that beside the King rode Stephen Langton, who was the Archbishop of Canterbury and one of the foremost of the leaders who had brought about this day. He saw, too, his own master, the Earl, advancing to meet the King, and many another bold and steadfast baron as well, who had staked his fortune and his life on this hour. The barons had won!

As for King John, Geoffrey stared in amazement to see how he spoke and joked, even laughed with those about him! He bowed graciously to someone in the crowd as though he felt no shame at being defeated by the nobles. But, just before he dismounted from his horse, Geoffrey saw the King's eyes dart to left and right among the crowd, and then across the river where, it was said, the few French troops that he had left were encamped.

Was he measuring the power of his army at the

last, desperate moment against that of his enemies? Whatever the King's thoughts, he gave no further sign of them. He swung from his saddle to the ground and walked between the armored ranks to the royal barge.

Like a flock of heavy, bright-feathered birds the barges swept out across the stream to the island. Again the crown waited; it seemed to hold its breath as it listened for the signal that would tell them that the Magna Carta had been signed and sealed. At last a trumpet call sounded over the water! And at that silver-pealing note a cry rose into the still summer air, a shout that became a roar of joy and triumph over Runneymede. The Great Charter had been signed!

Geoffrey, too, shouted and tossed his cap into the air with the rest of the crowd. But he knew as little as did any other how many centuries the echo of that shout would ring around the world!

Town Air is Free Air

DURING MOST of the Middle Ages, the people of Europe knew little or nothing about the world outside the small part of it in which they lived. They did not trade or visit with people of other countries as we do now. Their wants were simple, and each small community—farm, manor, or village—produced almost everything it needed.

But, about the time of the First Crusade, certain things happened which caused people to wish to know more about the world and to desire products and goods from other lands. Crusaders who traveled to the Holy Land brought back to their homes stories of the wonderful things they had seen in their journeys. They told of the spices, of the beautiful silks, and of the strange foods. Soon traders and merchants were bringing to Europe from Eastern lands, and from many other places, the wonderful things which were eagerly bought by those who had enough money to pay for them.

Because of the bad roads and the hard work of peddling wares from village to village and manor to manor, merchants found that fairs were the best places to sell goods. This is why, as you will see in the next story, fairs became such exciting and important places.

There is another way in which the Crusades

132

changed life in Europe. Because of the increased trade, cities and towns grew up. They became permanent places at which merchants and skilled workmen could sell their products. At first many of the people who lived in the towns were serfs, or slaves, of the lord who owned the land. But gradually these serfs became "free men." In the next story you will read more about how this change took place.

A S HE ran down the hill between the sun-baked barley fields, Jacques heard the sound of horse's hoofs behind him, and his heart beat faster in terror. Frantically he looked about for a hiding place. Once the Baron's game warden reached the top of the slope Jacques knew that he would be in plain sight, and he could never hope to run faster in the open than a man on horseback. If only there had been time to reach the forest!

And then he saw that the road before him dipped into a sharp little gully and crossed a low stone bridge before it mounted the other side. Here was his chance! With a final burst of speed he almost threw himself down the steep, rough back and under the bridge. There, knee-deep in water, he crouched and tried to quiet the gasps of breath that tore at his chest.

Pounding hoofs came nearer, thundered above his head, and faded into the distance. For this moment, at least, he was safe.

Suddenly a voice spoke, so near that Jacques's heart almost stopped in its wild beating. "Welcome, fellow traveler! Why so hurried in this midday heat?"

For a moment Jacques could not answer. He could only stare in fright at a man who sat on a stone under the shadow of the bridge. He was a stranger; that at least was comforting to the boy. Moreover, the man's sun-burned face was smiling. His clothes, though shabby and travel-stained, were made of gay and oddly combined colored pieces of cloth. Beside him lay a pack, and at his feet a small white dog with bright little eyes looked up at Jacques and wagged his tail.

"Well?" the stranger continued. "Have you nothing to say to me? And why were you running in that headlong fashion?"

Dared he tell? For a moment Jacques hesitated. He had met with little kindness in his eleven years, but something in the man's frank and friendly eyes gave him courage. "I was running from the Baron's game warden. I had meant no harm—truly! I was going to my work in the fields and as I passed a patch of young cabbage plants belonging to the Widow Yvonne, I saw a dear eating them. The Widow Yvonne was kind to me when—when my father and mother died, and I hated to see her crop spoiled. I only tried to frighten the deer away by throwing clods at it—not to hit it, mind you, for I know that that is forbidden. But I missed my aim and one clod struck the dear!"

The stranger's face grew grave. "And the game warden—he saw you?"

"Yes. He was riding through the fields a distance away, but he saw me. He shouted my name, and I ran. You see, the Baron, our master, is a famous hunter, and he has sworn that any serf who so much as touches one of his deer will not only be beaten, but will have his ears cut off as well! I have been flogged before—I could stand that! But the other...!

Jacques stopped speaking and caught his breath Well, he had given himself away now! Driven by some instinct he had put his fate into the hands of a man whom he had never seen before this moment! He waited, his eyes fixed desperately on the face in which he saw pity and indignation, but no horror at his crime, and no fear at all.

"But what did you hope to gain by running?" the man asked him. "Are you not a serf, bound to this minor? Will it not go harder with you than ever if you are caught?

"I thought that if I could reach the forest I might have a chance to hide there," said Jacques. He was thinking more clearly now, and the more he thought, the more hopeless everything seemed. A small boy alone in the forest with no weapon, not even a knife! It seemed a bitter choice that he must make—starvation or death from wild beasts in the forest, or the Baron's cruelty if he returned to the village!

The stranger was frowning intently and rubbing his chin. "No, not the forest," he said. "The thing for you to do, my boy, is to make your way to the town. If you can but reach the town you have a good chance to find shelter there. And if you remain there for a year and a day, neither the Baron nor all his soldiers can drag you back here again, for you will be a serf no longer, but a free man! The problem is how to get there!"

"I had not thought of that!" cried Jacques, his face suddenly lighting with hope. "I have heard that towns-people are free, not serfs. But I have never been half so far as that—I do not know the way. And besides, the Baron's men will be guarding the roads. He has never let a serf of his escape. He boasts of that far and wide!"

"He does, does he?" the man suddenly slapped his leg and turned to the pack beside him. "I have it!" Rummaging in its depths he brought out a bundle wrapped in many folds of bright cloth. "This will do the trick." Quickly he unwrapped the package. Inside a squat glass bottle containing a brownish liquid. He held it up, smiling. "This, my boy, is walnut stain, and this is what will save you. We will darken your skin with this and cover your yellow hair with a turban. You shall be a young Saracen slave who helps me with my juggling show. You see, I am Alard the Juggler. I am now on my way to the Fair there at the town, and often before I have dressed a young lad to play the part when I wished to give a special performance!"

"But..." began Jacques.

"No buts. This is your chance. Come off with your clothes and let me cover you well with this juice! Then with a costume out of my pack and a brown skin out of this bottle, the game warden can ride past in his

136

search and never suspect who you are in all the wide world. Once in the town, I'll lead you to a friend of mine who will be glad to take you in—that I can swear!"

Swiftly the juggler worked. The warm air dried the walnut stain rapidly. The little white dog, capering with excitement, was the only witness to the transformation of the fair-haired, brown-eyed French peasant boy into a dark little heathen in a purple turban and a long red gown. But they were none too quick, because Jacques had only just finished hiding his ragged, woolen tunic under some stones when horse's hoofs, approaching rapidly, warned them that the game warden was returning.

"Come!" said Alard. "Courage! Sit here in the shade. We are travelers resting and eating our midday meal. But remember! I will do all the talking, because you, my boy, cannot speak our language! Here, take this bread and eat!"

Jacques took the bread and obediently bit off a piece, but he was so frightened that he could not swallow it. The juggler, however, seemed to have no fear at all. Indeed he was smiling! A mischievous light danced in his eyes as he whispered to Jacques, "He's seen the bridge, and it has just occurred to him to look beneath."

Then came a shower of loose stones and dirt, and they saw the burly game warden guide his horse down the slope of the gully. When he saw them he reigned in abruptly. "Ho there!" he shouted. "You, under the bridge—come here! I want to speak with you!"

Alard rose to his feet, brushing the crumbs from his knees. "At your service, master," he said smoothly.

"Surely we are doing no harm here, myself and my blackamoor? The sun is so hot..."

"No, no!" said the game warden impatiently. "You may rest here for all of me! But tell me, did you see anything of a running cur of a peasant boy?"

"A small, thin lad? Yes, such a boy came scrambling down here only a short time ago," he answered the juggler.

"Which way did he run to?" shouted the horseman, as Alard paused again.

"Why it was comical!" Alard threw his head back and laughed long and heartily, while the impatient game warden waited. "He came tumbling in almost on top of us, but then one look at my Saracen was too much for him. He let out a shriek and ran! He must have thought him a demon risen out of the earth!"

"But which way did he run? Which way, man?"

"Why, up the gully, as fast as his legs would carry him!" said the juggler and pointed up the bed of the stream.

With an oath, the man turned his horse and forced the unwilling animal over the slippery rocks. In a moment he was out of sight.

Alard stood looking after him for a moment, then turned and sat down again, smiling. "Finish your dinner, my boy. You have nothing to fear now," he said.

Jacques obeyed and suddenly discovered how very hungry he was and how delicious were the crusty black bread and cheese that the juggler gave him. The man watched him eat, and produced another small loaf from his pack when Jacques had finished the first. "How long is it since you had your fill of food?" he asked gently.

"Had my *fill*?" Jacques opened his eyes wide. "Why—who ever has his fill, except when the Baron gives a feast and lets us peasants into the castle to celebrate too? There hasn't been one of those since last autumn. But," he added, "we always have *some* food here in our village, even throughout the winter. No one has starved to death here for a long time, not since three years ago when the Baron's enemies burned our crops and storehouses!"

To this Alard answered nothing, but sat waiting while Jacques ate the last crumb of the bread and cheese. The man's pleasant, open face had grown dark and serious. It contrasted strangely with his bright clothing. When the boy had finished, the juggler rose to his feet. "Well, shall we start on our journey?" he asked. Jacques rose also, stumbling awkwardly over the long robe.

Alard swung the pack to his shoulders. The little dog pranced gleefully ahead of them as they climbed the bank of the stream to the road. He stood at the top waiting and looking back to see which way they would turn.

"What do you call him?" Jacques asked as he stooped to pat the eager little nose.

"His name is Pierrot," said the juggler. "And he is fully as good an acrobat as I. Watch." He began to whistle a gay tune. The little dog stood erect on his hind legs and gravely circled around as though he were dancing. When the juggler took a bright-colored ball from his pack and tossed it to him, Pierrot caught it in his mouth and tossed it back without faltering in his dancing.

Jacques could hardly believe his eyes. "Oh" he gasped. "What a wonderful animal! Are you sure he is not bewitched?"

"You take the ball and toss it to him," said Alard. This Jacques did, and each time Pierrot returned it to him accurately.

"No, he is not bewitched," said the juggler when the performance was over. "I myself taught him the trick and many others as good or better. It takes patience and kindness, but no magic, I promise you. Come, take this cord and belt up that robe out of your way. We have six miles to go before we reach the town, and the only way to cover the miles is to set one foot bravely before the other!"

Along the road they went. The peasants paused in their work to stare at the travelers. But on no face, not even of those who knew him best, did Jacques see any sign of recognition! The juggler had done a good job of changing him from a French peasant boy! The game warden also passed them again, riding with a group of the Baron's men. They were looking for *him*, Jacques knew well!

The farther edge of the forest marked the boundary of the Baron's lands. Beyond this point neither Jacques nor any other of the serfs was allowed to go without special permission. Jacques had never been this far from his village before. A feeling of strangeness, a sort of desperate fear seized him as they left the narrow, rutted manor road and turned into a broad,

140

dusty highway that followed the poplar-lined curves of the river into the dim distance. And people were moving along the road—a great many people!

Alard could feel the boy's fear. "Come, freedom was never won by a faint heart!" he said. "There is nothing for you to be afraid of. If anyone speaks to you, you need only grin and bob your head. I'll tell you exactly what to do. Selim shall be your name—remember, Selim!"

It turned out exactly as the juggler had said. There were many travelers on the highway, all bound, just as they were, for the Fair. They stared at Jacques in open curiosity, but they seemed to believe without question the story that Alard told them of how the slave , Selim, had been captured by Crusaders in the Holy Land and purchased by Alard for a great price because he was supposed to be wise and clever at tricks. "But I had a bad bargain!" the juggler said, making a wry face. "Of all the stupid, useless heathens ever to come into a Christian land, he is the worst! Is it not so Selim?" and Jacques, taking Alard's cue, grinned and nodded his head with such a cheerful agreement that their fellow travelers laughed uproariously to see him.

The miles passed easily. Jacques, used to the hard long work in the fields, had no trouble in keeping up with the juggler's swinging stride. The sun was still high above the rim of hills when they came in sight at last of the end of their journey—the town! The first of it that Jacques saw was a high roof and two tall towers against the distant horizon. For the moment they were alone on the road together and Jacques could not speak without fear. "What is that?" he asked, stopping in his tracks.

"That?" The juggler followed his eyes and smiled. "That is the Cathedral of Our Lady, and it stands in the town that we are seeking. But it is built so tall that we can see it plainly from here, although the rest of the city is not yet in sight. If you have never seen a cathedral, you have something to look forward to! It is a wonder and a glory—a dwelling fit indeed for the Queen of Heaven! Towers and doors are richly decorated with the finest carved figures, but to my mind the inside is the most marvelous of all. The great windows are made of pieces of colored glass skillfully put together to form pictures of the Holy Scriptures and the lives of the Saints. When the sun shines through them, the colors are so beautiful that indeed I am sure that Paradise itself can be no more splendid!"

As they drew nearer, they could see the rest of the town. Most of the roofs were thatched, but a few were made of tiles. Soon they could see the walls that surrounded the town, with their many towers and battlements.

The road was now more crowded with travelers. There were peasants in their best holiday clothes; peddlers bent double under their packs; trains of pack-horses carrying goods to sell at the Fair; farm carts loaded with produce; now and then a rich traveler—noble or churchman or merchant—riding on a fine horse or mule, with his servant behind. Alard spoke gaily and cheerfully to all; he was a general favorite, Jacques could see clearly, and was known for his wit and fun as well as for his skill in juggling.

A thought had occurred to Jacques, and as soon as there was a chance to speak, he asked a question. "Why is it that these townspeople are free, as you say? Surely they are not all nobly born?"

"No," answered the juggler. "They were but poor folk — serfs also — to begin with. This city was a village much like yours long ago. But because it lay beside this river and because the shrine of the Saint in whose honor the city is named, from its beginning many travelers passed through it. It became a good place at which to trade goods. Even the poor folk were able to save a little for themselves beyond what was claimed in taxes by their feudal lord, the bishop.

"Then, years ago, the ruling bishop decided to make a pilgrimage to the Holy Land for the good of his soul. Since he had not money enough to go in the lordly style he wished, he went to the shopkeepers and asked them to give him, as a favor, money beyond what was the lawful tax due him. They replied that they would give it to him gladly if in return he would grant them a charter — a promise that they could form a free district or commune, that they would no longer be serfs but free men. He signed the charter, and thus it was that the serfs bought their freedom from serfdom.

"Since then the commune of the town has bought many more liberties at other prices from other bishops, but that was the beginning. Only lately, so I hear, the duke of the province wished to give a new chapel to Our Lady's Cathedral, and the stonecutters and glass-makers who are at work on it had his promise, in return, that the goods they wished to ship in boats are to be carried down the river through all his lands, free of toll, or tax.

Now they had reached a spot which overlooked the valley in which the town was situated. Outside the walls the meadows stretched along beside the river. These meadows were so thickly covered with bright-colored tents, booths, and pavilions that they looked like a garden gay with flowers.

"This is the Fair," said the juggler, pointing to the meadows. "Every summer at this time they hold the Fair here, outside the walls of the town. People come here from miles away—even from far countries. They trade and buy and sell here for three weeks; then they move on to the next Fair, which is held in another city. I think from the looks of it that it is a larger Fair than ever before."

Even to those who had seen such a Fair before, it was a brilliant sight, but to Jacques's eyes, it was little short of a miracle! Each booth or stall or tent seemed to be trying to outdo the next in color. Flags and banners waved in the wind, and, as the two travelers drew nearer, a steady sound came to meet them. When they reached the edge of the Fair, the noise became almost deafening as each merchant or huckster proclaimed to the crowd how fine were the goods that he offered for sale.

Back and forth, in and out, through the streets of this city of tents outside the town walls, pushed the crowds. Such crowds, all dressed in their gayest and best! There were townsfolk and peasants, rich and poor,

144

noble and common, soldiers and churchmen, merchants and beggars, men, women, and children. Beyond the fair grounds, on the sparkling blue water of the river, the barges of the merchants tugged at their moorings as the current moved swiftly under them. There was trading and bargaining going on everywhere. Now and then a group of constables would hurry through the crowd to settle a dispute that threatened to become a real battle. But to Jacques it seemed as though most of the people were out here merely for enjoyment—to laugh, gossip, and admire the displays spread to catch their attention.

And such displays! Along one row of booths were shown all sorts and varieties of the weaver's art. Cloth from the coarsest woolen to the finest linen from Flanders,[1] silk from the East, velvets from Italy! Another group of shops displayed metal dishes—gleaming copper kettles and pots and iron cooking vessels of every shape and size. Here was a row of stands selling pottery, there another offering leather goods, and there another filled with glassware. A strange-looking man in a turban much like the one that Jacques was wearing offered bundles of sweat-smelling herbs and pungent spices. At another booth a group of monks and priests were absorbed in looking over finished books with fresh white parchment leaves.

Trying to see everything at once, Jacques began to lag farther and farther behind his guide. "On my word!" laughed the juggler as he stopped to wait for him. "You

1. A region lying within Belgium, the Netherlands, and France.

are forgetting your reason for coming on this journey. And look at my poor Pierrot! He is tired and the crowds frighten him. Pick him up, and come along!"

Jacques gathered the little dog into his arms and followed the tall figure of the juggler through the crowds. It was true; he had forgotten that he was still in great danger!

Just as they were nearing the gate of the city where the great drawbridge lay across the moat, the crowd began to move hurriedly aside to make way for a group of passing horsemen. Looking up, Jacques almost let Pierrot fall, for at the head of the company rode his own master, the Baron! Behind him came a group of his squires and soldiers, most of whose faces were familiar to Jacques. If Jacques could have done so through the walnut stain, he would have turned pale in that moment! And his terror increased when he saw the Baron pull his horse in abruptly. Then, to his unspeakable relief, he saw that his master was looking at Alard and not at him.

"You there, fellow!" cried the Baron. His rough, brutal face was, for once, wearing a jolly expression. "Are you not the juggler who was here at the Fair last year?"

Alard took off his cap and bowed low. "Yes, my Lord Baron," he answered. "It is gracious of you to remember me!"

The Baron turned to another richly dressed horseman at his side. "This is the man I was telling you of. He kept six balls in the air, I say, and threw them back and forth to his dog all at the same time. You would

146

not believe me, but now I can prove it!" Then to Alard he said, "Do that same juggling trick now and I'll pay you well. But if you fumble and make me lose my wager, you'll smart for it!"

The crowd, delighted at the prospect of a show, made a space about Alard. At first Jacques was so paralyzed with fear that he could only stand and clutch Pierrot against him. But when Alard clapped him briskly on the shoulder and whispered, "Courage!" in his ear, he began to recover himself. After all, wasn't it really funny to be putting on a performance in front of his own cruel master, who gave the turbaned little Saracen no more than a passing glance?

And in a moment Jacques, like the crowd, became breathless at the skill and grace with which his friend the juggler tossed colored ball after colored ball into the air! It seemed unbelievable, but there really were six balls all flashing there in the sunshine!

"Bravo! Bravo!" cried the Baron, and the crowd, too, clapped and cheered. And then, at a whistle from Alard, little Pierrot wriggled out of Jacques's arms and began his slow, solemn dance to the lively air his master was whistling. One after another, he caught the balls in his mouth as they were tossed to him; with a flip of his head he sent them to Jacques. He, in turn, threw them to the juggler who whirled them into the air again! And when it was over Alard bowed to the ground, Pierrot crouched with his nose between his two front paws, and Jacques, at a hint from the juggler, bobbed his head and grinned his broadest grin!

"Bravo!" cried the Baron again, and tossed a jingling purse which Alard caught deftly. A scattering of smaller coins came from the watching crowd. Alard bowed his thanks while picking up the coins to put in the pouch that hung from his belt. When the group of horsemen had moved on once more and the crowd had closed in about the three performers, the juggler did not speak. But, by the way he wiped his sleeve across his forehead and rolled his eyes, Jacques knew that he had realized the danger in which they had both stood! Aiding a serf to escape was as severely punished as stealing.

While he followed Alard over the drawbridge and under the huge stone archway of the city gate, Jacques was troubled by the thought that Alard was in danger too, and because of him. Fear for himself had filled his mind so completely that he had not even considered the risk he was bringing on this man who had taken pity on him. And the other—the juggler's friend to whom they were now going. Would he be in danger too? There was a reward offered, Jacques knew, for anyone who might return a runaway serf to his master. Alard would never betray him, but what of this other man? What reason would he have for helping an unknown peasant boy who had not the slightest claim on his protection and sympathy?

These were sobering and unhappy ideas to carry through the gaiety and bustle that filled the narrow streets within the city walls. How close together the houses were, and how tall! Some of them were as much as three or even four stories high, and each story overhung the next, so that in places the two rows of houses almost met and all but shut out the sky! Through narrow doorways and small, barred windows came gleams of candlelight. The sun had not gone down, yet the houses were already dark within. Smells of cooking filled the air and reminded Jacques that in spite of his good meal at noon, his long walk had given him a keen appetite again. Pigs, dogs, and chickens scurried about through the unpaved streets, hunting for whatever they could find to eat among the garbage and waste thrown out-of-doors by housewives. If it were not for the cleaning done by the animals, the street would be impassible indeed!

How in the world could Alard tell where he was going? Jacques was almost dizzy with following the twisting, curving streets, each one so much like the next. But at last the juggler stopped before a door and rapped with his knuckles. Jacques waited, his heart beating fast, to see the person who was to give him shelter for the coming year and a day!

The door opened to disclose a small, bent man, not in the least like Alard. He was dressed neatly in shabby dark clothes and a close-fitting, hood-like cap covered his hair. His face was dark and thin and marked with deep lines; his eyes were deep-set and piercing. But when he recognized Alard there appeared on his face an unexpectedly bright and gentle smile. "Welcome!" he cried, throwing open the door wide. "Come in, my friend! I was hoping that the Fair would bring you to my door again!"

They followed their host into a small room where a cheerful fire glowed on the hearth. The pot that hung above it was sending out jets of steam and a delicious odor. "Welcome," repeated the man again, as he moved two more stools close to the rough wooden table that was set before the fire.

The juggler slipped his pack from his back and Pierrot, leaping from Jacques's arms, began to show frantic delight at finding an old friend. "Pierrot has not changed!" said their host. "But who is this?" He looked curiously at Jacques. "No Saracen, I can see that plain enough!"

Alard smiled. "Your eyes are keen, friend Gervais![1] Lucky for him that others were not so good as yours." Then, without further delay, he told of Jacques's escape and flight, omitting no smallest detail. "And I have told him," concluded the juggler, "that you, of all the men I know, were the one whom we could surely trust to give him shelter and help for the year and a day until he shall be free."

Master Gervais paused in his petting of Pierrot. He looked into the boy's eyes, where hope and fear showed so plainly. "Alard is right," he said. "No doubt you are wondering how he can be so sure that I will help you." Reaching up, he removed the cap from his head, and Jacques saw that where his ears should have been there were only long-healed scars. "Now you know," he said, smiling his gentle smile and replacing his cap. "But I was not so lucky as you—I did not learn in time the truth of the saying, 'Town air is free air.' You are welcome, my boy. I am a poor man, but if you are willing to help me at

1. Pronounced: *Zhervay.*

my work, I have enough to keep us both."

"There! I almost forgot!" Alard tossed something upon the table, something that clinked as it struck. It was the Baron's purse. "Here is a little silver that Jacques's master gave him!" He winked gaily at the boy. "An appetite like his would soon eat you out-of-doors without some such help! Now for supper! That soup smells too good to waste away in steam!"

Three wooden bowls were filled, and a small bowl of food was given to Pierrot. Three wooden spoons were soon at work. Not before, however, three heads had bowed over the table to give a grateful thanks to Heaven for the food and for the freedom to be won in this town, freedom that was far more precious than any food or drink could be!

Marco and the Marble Hand

IN THE LAST PART of the Middle Ages, the city of Florence, in the part of Italy called Tuscany, was the center of a new interest in books, in painting, in sculpture, and in architecture. From the time that the Roman Empire was destroyed (see the first story) until about the thirteenth century, the Christian Church was the only center of learning; the priests and monks were the only teachers. Then in Italy a great change began to take place. Because of the large amount of business which the Italian merchants did, they became very wealthy. This wealth gave them much free time to use in studying music, art, and literature. Many people began to read old Greek and Roman books, to see the ancient pictures and statues, and to learn about how the non-Christian peoples had lived. Before this time anything which was not Christian had been considered worthless.

At this time artists began to paint pictures of people and scenes in everyday life, not just of saints and of religious scenes. These new pictures were eagerly bought by the rich merchants. Soon good artists became respected and famous persons, and some of them became quite wealthy.

In the next story you will read about how seriously a small peasant boy who lived near Florence took this new interest in art and education.

"ARCO! Marco!"

Marco buried his head deeper into the covers to shut out the sound of his mother's voice. But it continued. Someone began to shake him by the shoulder. "Wake up, sleepy-head! Have you forgotten that this is market day?"

Then Marco was wide awake in an instant! He sat up and blinked the sleep from his eyes. By the flickering rush light which his mother held in her hand he saw that she was laughing down into his face. "Wake up!" she repeated. "Your father is hitching Beppo to the cart. Do you want him to go without you?" Then she hurried away, taking the light with her.

Marco pulled on his clothes as fast as he could. He was shivering partly with cold and partly with excitement. For Marco, dressing meant only slipping into his hairy goatskin breeches, tucking his shirt inside them, and pulling his best doublet of green Cambrai cloth over his head. He ran down the steep inside stairs that led from the second-floor living quarters of the house to the stables, storerooms, cow stalls, and wagon sheds below. Although it was midsummer, the stone steps felt icy cold to his bare feet.

A lantern with sides made of transparent horn of a sheep hung on the wall. By its light Marco could see that the heavy, nail-studded doors of the house stood open to the night. Beppo, their small white horse, was already harnessed to the two-wheeled cart that was to carry their load of farm produce and themselves into the market place of the great city of Florence.

Marco's father, Piero Cavazzo, was an honest, hard-working peasant who rented his land from the owner, a wealthy wool merchant in the city of Florence. Usually he sent one of his two older sons to market, for he himself disliked to take the time from his work to make the long journey. But on the last trip young Giovanni had not got for the produce the prices that his shrewd father had expected. Piero, therefore, was going today to do the bargaining himself. Marco, the youngest of his boys, had finally got his consent to go along.

From the little country village where they lived to the city was a long drive. If they were to enter the gates of Florence at sunrise, they must start long before dawn. Only by being there just as the gates opened could they hope to get the most favorable spot in the market square in which to display what they had to sell.

Piero appeared suddenly in the doorway from the darkness outside. He looked twice his normal size in his bulky sheepskin coat. "All ready, Marco? Where is the basket of eggs? I thought I told you to put it in the cart last night?"

Marco's heart began to race wildly, but he kept his voice steady. So his father had noticed that the basket was missing! "Here it is, father. I left it here on the stone shelf to keep cool. I wasn't going to forget!"

"Well, mind you hold it carefully! Those eggs should bring a good price from Master Antonio's workshop," said his father as Marco brought the basket into the lantern light. "We're fortunate to have so good a customer. He is a fine painter and one of the great men of Florence!" He lifted the lantern down from its hook on the wall and hung it on the short pole that stood up from one corner of the cart. Then he climbed to the seat.

Marco climbed in also and found a comfortable spot among the sacks of cabbages, the pairs of big, solid cheeses, the jars of olive oil, the baskets of fruit, the carefully tied bundles of sweet-smelling herbs, and the woven willow hamper that contained his mother's chief pride, the pats of cream cheeses lovingly packed in fresh green rushes. With a creek and clatter of wheels the cart jerked forward and out into the empty dark street that ran through the little huddle of houses that was their village on the hilltop.

Down the short stretch of steep cobblestones they drove. The high walls on either side echoed back each rattle and squeak of the wooden wheels. Marco looked up to where the stars showed, bright and clear, in the narrow crack of sky between the overhanging roofs.

Those same stars were shining down now on the towers and battlements of Florence. When the sun rose, he, Marco, would be there in the marvelous "City of the Red Lilies." He would soon be part of the busy, brilliant crowds. To a small boy of fourteenth-century Tuscany, Florence was the center of the whole world.

The walls gave back a different echo as they passed under the little arched gateway of the village. Then they were suddenly out in the great empty darkness of the countryside, with the whole wide canopy of sky stretched above their heads. Marco's hand tightened on the handle of the basket of eggs. If all went well, he might not be returning when this cart rolled under the archway again! The thought made him breathe faster and gave him a fluttering, hollow feeling inside. How *could* he bear the waiting to learn whether or not his plan would work? He mustn't think of the basket, he decided, or the secret that lay hidden under the smooth brown and white eggs! He must think about something else — anything else. He lay back and looked up at the stars again. It seemed to him that they were friendly, twinkling eyes, smiling down upon him.

Marco must have fallen asleep, because the next thing that he knew the stars were only pale pin-points in a graying sky. He sat up and saw that behind the line of mountains in the east the dawn was painting the sky with fire. Beside the road the olive trees had turned from clumps of inky shadow to silvery green, and in every single one of them birds were singing.

Piero Cavazzo, hunched sleepily over the reins,

straightened up and clucked to his horse as they began to overtake and pass others who were on their way to market. Some drove loaded mules or pack-horses; others rode in carts behind slow, patient oxen. Here and there a peddler walked, bent under the pack on his back, or a full-skirted peasant woman, erect and proud as a queen, stepped along with a basket balanced on her head. Soon the road became so crowded that there was no room for Beppo, their sturdy little horse, to pass others. Marco and his father had to be content to follow the cart just ahead of them. The line seemed to drag along like a slow, dusty serpent. Marco, standing up to look ahead, was thankful to see that, although they were not the very first, there were only a few others who would reach the market place ahead of them.

They reached the top of a long hill and then started down the other side. In the distance, between lines of poplar trees, the river Arno flashed briefly, only to disappear again among the crowded houses of the suburbs of Florence. And just as the sun finally appeared above the hills, Piero drew rein under the high towers and walls of Florence.

Grumbling as always, Piero Cavazzo searched for soldi in the purse that hung by his belt. These small coins he must give to the guards for permission to enter the city. Slowly the gates creaked open, each man paid his toll, and the wheels rumbled over the drawbridge across the moat, and through the second gateway into the waking city.

As if to greet the newcomers, from every one of

the towers and pinnacles, from everywhere that a bell could be hung, came the sound of chimes. The air seemed to shake with the lovely sound. Pigeons, startled from their roosts, filled the same air with the whirl of their white and silver wings.

Marco looked about at the crowds of people that began to fill the narrow streets. How gaily they were dressed, how differently from the peasants of his village! Everyone, rich or poor, seemed to be trying to get as many different colors and materials as he could into one costume. Only the friars, the priests, and the nuns, it seemed, were content with sober grays and blacks and browns.

He looked up at the high buildings whose walls were dark and grim in the fresh morning sun. Behind those barred windows were the rich and luxurious palaces of the nobles and the great merchants who had made the name of Florence known far and wide. Even as far as the northern sea-island of England Florence was famous! From that island came the wool that, woven into cloth and dyed to brilliant colors, now hung drying on long lines across these same streets.

Now they had reached the river Arno, and were crossing it on the crowded Ponte Vecchio.[1] The merchants whose shops lined this old bridge were not yet ready for business. Only a few sleepy apprentices were beginning to unbar the doors and open the shutters as the carts rolled past. Marco recognized among them a boy from his own village. This boy had been taken in

1. *Ponte* is the Italian word for bridge.

as an apprentice to learn the trade of a goldsmith. Marco shouted his name, and the boy's face, as he answered, showed delight at seeing an old friend. Marco wondered suddenly if it were possible to be homesick for one's quiet village in the midst of the marvelous color and excitement of Florence! Once again his hand tightened its grip on the handle of the basket.

At last Piero Cavazzo reined in his horse and the cart came to a stop in the open space of the vegetable market. After backing into the spot he had selected, Piero began to rearrange his wares so they would show to the best advantage. "Put the basket of eggs down here for the time being," he told his son. "And then take Beppo and water him. Hurry, because I want you to lose no time in getting those eggs to Master Antonio."

Marco needed no urging to make him hurry, but old Beppo seemed to feel, not unjustly, that since his labors were over there was no need for haste. He drank slowly and with the greatest relish. While the horse paused for long breaths Marco impatiently stood first on one foot, then on another. What if his father should decide to change the eggs to another basket? The thought turned him cold! But when he returned, the basket was just as he left it. Piero was deep in a discussion on the merits of his cheeses with a portly citizen in a red and black hood.

"Be off with you on your errand. I'll give the horse his grain," he told Marco briefly and returned to his customer.

Master Antonio's workshop lay in another section of the city, but Marco knew the way well. He had gone there several times before with his father or his older brothers to take the eggs that the painter needed for mixing his colors. Master Antonio was a careful craftsman, and to his mind there was a great deal of difference in the mixing qualities of eggs. Marco, listening eagerly, had heard the master tell his apprentices that they should always get their eggs from one place. Then they would find their colors were always the same. "And moreover," he warned them, "be sure that you use only those eggs with the palest yellow yolks when mixing colors to paint the flesh of children and young women. Save the darker yolks for the weathered skins of men and older people. All these things must be watched, if you are to reach perfection!"

The memory of the fascinations of that workshop made Marco's cheeks burn with excitement, and he hurried his steps. Through the crowded, narrow streets he walked as fast as he could, but always he shielded his precious burden from the pushing passers-by. Then as he came out into a small piazza, or square, he stopped in surprise. Men in the gay uniform of one of the princely houses that faced the square were sweeping the cobblestones. Others, perched on ladders, were draping long festoons and wreaths of leaves and flowers along the facade[1] of the palace. A group of carpenters was busily hammering at a wooden platform that was to fill one corner of the square. Another group

1. The front of a building.

struggled with the poles of a striped canopy which billowed in the wind and almost fell and covered them in its folds.

"What's going on here?" asked Marco of a friendly faced woman who stood among the crowd of onlookers.

"Don't you know?" exclaimed the woman in surprise. Then she glanced down at Marco. His dark curls, his eager, sunburnt face, the goatskin breeches made him look for all the world like one of the fauns carved by the ancient sculptors. "Oh, I see, your a country lad. Well, they're preparing for a wedding feast. Monna Lisabette, the daughter of the rich old Ser Casoli, is to be married. There will be processions and entertainments, music and dancing in the street, and feasting—such feasting for all! They say that Ser Casoli has fifty cooks and twenty confectioners already at work! It will be well worth your while to be on hand, I can tell you!"

But the weight of the basket of eggs on his arms and the heavier burden of the secret it contained seemed more important to Marco than cooks and confectioners. He hurried on through the square and was soon in another labyrinth of crooked, dark streets. Here the cobbles were stained to brilliant colors by the waste that the wool dyers constantly poured into the streets from their vats. It was like walking over rainbows, and more pleasant to eyes and nose than the next street where the bloody refuse from the butcher shops was fought over in the gutters by hoards of stray dogs who growled as Marco passed.

Coming into another small square, Marco was aware at once of the heavy silence of the place. Here there was a fear, a tension and uneasiness on the faces of the people. There was no talk or chatter or crying of wares! Following the anxious eyes of the crowd, Marco saw across the square a group of young men in bright-colored clothes walk slowly out into the sunshine from the heavy, shadowed doorway of one of the palaces. Another group, differently dressed, advanced across the open space to meet them. They stalked over the cobbles with the stiff, arrogant manner of angry bulldogs. Their hands were ready on the hilts of their swords.

Marco paused and watched with the rest of the crowd. He had seen enough of street fights to recognize this as the beginning of one. "Who are they?" he whispered to a ragged street urchin who balanced impatiently up and down on his toes as though eager for the fray to begin.

"Those coming out of the gateway are the Albizzi, and the others, who wear the red balls embroidered on cloth of gold, are the Medici.[1] The Albizzi have lorded it in these streets long enough. I hope the other men will teach them that Florence is no place for aristocrats. It is a free city!" said the boy fiercely.

He turned as he spoke and looked at Marco, then at the basket of eggs. An expression of impish mischief crossed his dirty face. Before Marco could move to stop him, he had snatched an egg and hurled it at the

1. Pronounced *Medichi.*

162

swarthy, hawk-nosed leader of the Albizzi. His aim was good; the egg struck the man full in the face!

There was a startled scream from a woman some-where in the crowd, and an oath of rage from the man as the egg dripped stickily down his face. Then the onlookers scattered like leaves in the wind before the rush of the armed bravos. After one horror-stricken instant Marco took to his heels with the rest. The black anger in the man's face and the bare sword in his hand warned Marco that, once he was caught with his bas-ket, there would be no time for him to explain that *he* had not thrown the egg. And he would *not* drop his basket!

Angry shouts behind him and the sound of steel on steel told him that the young firebrands of the Midici party had wasted no time in getting into the fight. Luck-ily for Marco, two of them overtook his pursuer just as the man had all but trapped him behind one of the pil-lars of the arched loggia.[1] When the Albizzi turned to defend himself, Marco dashed for the corner and down the next street. He put as much distance as he could between himself and the quarrel that continued in the square.

At last, in a quiet little alley near the river, he came to the sprawling, barn-like wooden building that housed the bottega, or workshop, of Master Antonio. Still breathing hard, Marco knocked at the door. It was opened by Taddeo, the fat old porter whom Marco knew well. "You're late!" said Taddeo, trying to make his

---

1. A roofed open gallery, a kind of porch.

voice sound severe. But then his round, red face grew more kindly. "What has happened? You look as though you had seen a ghost!"

"They were fighting in the piazza back there," Marco told him. "Someone in the crowd threw one of my eggs at a soldier, and he chased me."

Instead of showing sympathy, Taddeo burst into a guffaw of laughter. "I suppose that somebody wasn't you? Oh, *no* indeed!" he said, with a huge wink. "Well, the Albizzi and the Medici are at it again, I expect. When you're as old as I, you'll learn not to mix in such affairs."

Marco's face flushed, but he didn't try to argue or explain. The danger was past, and he had something vastly more important on his mind. "I want to speak to Master Antonio, if you please," he said.

Taddeo suddenly grew pompous and important. "What do you want with him?" he asked. "Master Antonio is a great man, a busy man. I have the money for your eggs ready in my purse. Give them to me and be off with you." He held out his hand for the basket.

"No!" Marco said, drawing back. "I want to see Master Antonio himself because I have something else for him."

"Well, well, give to me and I will see that it comes to him!" said Taddeo impatiently.

But Marco stood his ground. "It is for him alone," he said. "It is something that I know he will be glad to see."

"I tell you the master is not to be disturbed!"

Taddeo was beginning to bluster again when there was a step behind him. The fine white head and rosy face of the old painter himself appeared in the doorway.

"Ah, the smallest Cavazzo and a basket of good country eggs. Come in my boy! What is it you wish to show me?" he asked kindly.

Marco followed Master Antonio into the big, dim room full of busy workers, boys, young men, and older men too. Some were grinding colors; some were mixing them in small earthenware pots; some were planing down boards of fine-grained linden wood to use for panel painting; others were rubbing chalk into the smooth surfaces of the boards as the final preparation for drawing. In a dusty shaft of sunlight that fell through one of the high windows a group was clustered round an ancient bronze statue. It was green with age and lacked a head. Nevertheless one of the apprentices was carefully measuring it and writing down the figures in a small notebook; others were sketching it from different angles.

Fascinated, Marco stood staring about him until Master Antonio's voice interrupted him. "Well, my boy. What is it?"

Then Marco began to lift the eggs carefully from his basket into the great stone jar that stood waiting for them. When the last one was out, he removed also a layer of the clean yellow straw that filled the bottom of the basket. "This is what I have brought you, sir," he said.

Master Antonio looked at what lay on the bright

straw and he drew in his breath. Carefully, reverently he lifted out a fragment of marble, softly mellowed by time to the color of warm old ivory. It was a marble hand! He held it up to the light and turned it this way and that. It was made of marble, yes, but so cleverly and skillfully formed that it seemed as through the tapering, delicate fingers and sensitive palm must be made of soft, living flesh. "Where did you get this, Marco?" asked Master Antonio gravely.

"I found it beside a brook where the ground was washed away by the spring floods. It was the only part broken off of the whole statue," said Marco.

The workmen, young painters, and apprentices, who had gathered silently around their master, exchanged looks. "A whole statue?" repeated Master Antonio. "Can you tell me what it was like?"

"It is a woman's figure, I think. I didn't dare to dig it out, because I feared someone might see it. My father believes what Brother Lucca, the parish priest, has told us. He says that all such ancient statues are heathen idols and must be destroyed. But I had seen those that you have here in your workshop, and I know they are too beautiful to be lost!" said Marco earnestly. "I couldn't see it all, but I did uncover the other arm. I can draw that for you if you wish."

One of the apprentices put the half-finished panel he was carrying into the boy's hand, and another gave him a piece of charcoal. Marco made a few strokes. Then, frowning and holding his tongue between his teeth, he set down on the wood the lovely curves and outlines as he remembered seeing them there on the dark, moist earth. He had remembered well the arm and the hand that held an apple in its outstretched palm. So intent was Marco that he did not see the eyes of the master meet those of his oldest pupil, above the boy's head.

"An ancient statue of Greek or Roman workmanship!" said Master Antonio. "A rare and precious treasure indeed to find in the earth! Only the ignorant and unlearned, nowadays, fear such things as idols! As you say, they are too beautiful to be destroyed, when we have so much to learn from them! You were a wise lad to come here to me with your news, and you shall be well rewarded. If you lead me to the place where the statue is, I shall give you this gold florin for your own." Master Antonio looked down into the boy's face with shrewd, twinkling eyes.

Marco looked at the bright coin. Never before in all his life had such a sum been within his own reach. But he put his hands behind him and backed away. "No, I thank you, master. I want no money, and I will lead you there whenever you say. But there is something else that I want, if it please you."

"Yes?" The smile in the old eyes deepened.

"I want to come here and work in your bottega, to learn to draw, to become a painter!" said Marco in a rush of words. Then as he stood looking up into the great man's face, his own face grew pale under its tan, so great was his wish and the terror that his boldness might have made the master angry.

And to Marco's great amazement and delight,

Master Antonio clapped an arm about his shoulders. "Good lad! I knew what you wanted as soon as I saw you draw with the charcoal on the wood! Yes, I'll take you in. I'm a hard taskmaster, but my boys here seem to thrive on it, and we have room for another with fingers like yours. Here, take the money for the eggs to your father, and bring him back to see me. We'll have the apprenticeship papers ready for him to sign this very day!"

And Marco ran back through the narrow streets of Florence as though his feet had wings.

A *Noble Magic*

DURING THE MIDDLE AGES there were very few books. The only way to make books was to write them by hand. Monks had to work long and hard as scribes, copying the books by hand on parchment. In more than one European country the books which were kept in the monasteries were the only books in that country.

Slowly the need and the demand for books became greater. After a time religious books were not the only ones desired. Then other men than monks became skilled as scribes in copying. Still there were not books enough for everyone. Only those who were rich could afford to buy the costly manuscripts.

Sometimes the pages of books were printed by means of wooden blocks, but these blocks were hard to make. Each block was carved to print one page. A set of blocks could be used for printing copies of only one book. The blocks did not last very long. Then a wonderful invention was made. That invention gave bookmakers a new way of printing. It made it possible for us to have the many books and libraries we have now. A man named Gutenberg, who lived in Germany five hundred years ago, is said to have invented the new method of printing. It is a method of printing about which you will read in the next story.

In "A Noble Magic" you will also read something about guilds and apprentices. The workers in each craft, or skilled industry, were organized into a guild. The members of a guild prepared their goods and sold them. Usually they sold the goods to the people who used them. A worker could become a member of a guild only after a long period of training or apprenticeship. To get this training a boy was apprenticed to a member, or master, of the guild which he wished to join. Often the boy's father had to pay the master a sum of money for the training. The apprentice lived with the master during the time of his training. When an apprentice finished his work, he became a journeyman, or free worker. But before he could become a master, he had to pass very strict examinations before members of the guild.

In the next story you will learn about a boy who did not wish to be a scribe and who found work for himself as an apprentice in a different trade.

THE afternoon sun streamed in through the low window, and with it came all the many sounds of a busy city, sounds that were fascinating to the years of a twelve-year-old boy. Karl shifted his position on the high stool, dipped his quill pen into the ink-pot on his desk, and bent over the page before him. And then, in spite of himself, his gaze wandered once more away from his task to the color and excitement that were visible through the open window.

This time he could see a company of guards in the bright-colored uniform of the Prince-Bishop of Strasbourg. They were on their way to Mass in the Cathedral. How they swaggered as they walked! How their long swords swung at their sides!

For a moment the narrow, cobbled street was empty; then it was filled once more. Now a noisy group of apprentices in leathern aprons and jaunty caps walked by. At the same time, from the other direction, came three fresh-cheeked market girls. When the two groups met, their gaiety and laughter echoed back and forth from the overhanging walls of the houses. After their passing, the street was so silent that Karl could almost fancy that he heard the rushing of the great river Rhine as it swept under the arches of the bridge.

Again he bent over his desk, but by this time the ink had dried on his pen. He wiped the quill carefully, to rid it of lumps, and dipped it once more. Then, with his tongue held between his teeth, he set to his task again of copying the beautiful, even, black letters from the manuscript page left by his Uncle Otto as a model for the work.

His page filled, Karl straightened to look it over. Alas! Even he could see how far it was from perfection! His letter E's, for instance, were still hopelessly uneven. And there were so many of them! So many E's on every page to be written over and over again in exactly the same way! Well, Uncle Otto would not be pleased with *this* sample of his work! He must get another one finished before his uncle's return for supper. Judging by the long shadows outdoors, he had not much more time.

But first he *had* to get the stiffness out of his muscles! He slipped from the stool and stretched his arms above his head luxuriously, yawning at the same time.

And just at this unlucky moment the door opened to show Uncle Otto's bent figure peering at him nearsightedly from the threshold! Flushing scarlet, Karl stopped in the middle of his yawn.

"So!" cried Uncle Otto. "So this is the way you spend your time! Let's see your paper there, my young sleepy-head!" He snatched the sample from Karl's hand and looked it over hastily. "Just as I thought! Scarcely better than when you first came here from the country! How can you expect to become even so much as an apprentice scribe, if you spend your time stretching and yawning!"

Karl knew how useless it was to make excuses. He hung his head and waited silently for his Uncle's anger to wear itself out.

"It was only as a favor to your poor mother that I took you in at all!" the old man continued in a sharper voice. "I doubted from the first that I could make anything out of such a clumsy peasant! How your parish

172

priest ever came to praise your work at his school so highly, I cannot even imagine! But no one can say that I did not do my Christian duty! I even got a promise from my master, the Reverend Prior Paul, that he would give you work as an apprentice in his library as soon as I thought you skillful enough to be useful. But mark my words! I shan't keep you here longer, eating at my expense and wasting costly paper, unless you work harder!"

"I have tried my best, uncle," said Karl, daring to speak at last. "I only just now got down off the stool because I was stiff from sitting still so long. At home, my work in the fields was different..."

"Well, if you want exercise, go build up the fire and get my supper!" said Uncle Otto in a gentler tone, his bad humor finally calmed.

Karl did as he was told. But as he warmed the thick pea soup and set out the bowls and cut the crusty black bread, his thoughts were rebellious. It wasn't the sitting still, merely, that was hard for him. The work itself seemed to him to so senselessly monotonous! Making the same little black marks over and over, day after day, week after week, year after year! It was no life for a man!

How much better he would have liked almost any other sort of labor! If, for instance, he could be apprenticed to a carpenter, a stonecutter, an armorer—even a blacksmith! He was strong and active and skillful with his hands. He could do well at any such work. But here in Strasbourg it seemed there was little chance for an outsider to be taken into any of the guilds that controlled those crafts. The number of apprentices in each guild was closely regulated. Karl knew that he was lucky to have the opportunity, through his uncle, of learning a trade that would earn him as good a living as the skilled copyists were making.

The whole world seemed to be wanting books, these days, and the labor of copying them out by hand was slow. Karl could well understand *why* so many people wanted books! Ever since he had learned to read he had felt that taking up a new book was like entering a new world. And no wonder copyists were well paid when books were so expensive! Why, Uncle Otto had told him that a plain Bible, without binding or colored initial letters, would cost as much as sixty guilders![1]

And there *was* one thing about being a copyist that would be very pleasant. A copyist, working in a library full of books, would be allowed to read. He could read those costly, beautiful manuscript books—things which no poor person could ever hope to own for himself!

As Karl was ladling the soup into bowls, a knock sounded on the door. Uncle Otto opened it to admit one of his friends, a rosy-faced old man named Peter.

"Come in! Come in!" cried Uncle Otto. "Karl, set another bowl and bring a chair to the table."

Master Peter rubbed his hands together. "The soup smells delicious—yes, I'll take a small portion, a small portion!" he said. Then, as he seated himself, he leaned

1. About twenty-five dollars [1942 dollars].

174

close to Uncle Otto. "I've heard some news!" he whispered.

"News? What news?"

"Strange news, indeed!" Master Peter nodded mysteriously. He blew into his hot soup, tasted it cautiously, then continued. "Yes! You remember what we were talking about the other day—of the strange doings of one John Gutenberg? About his locked and barred workshop and the closed-mouthed journeymen who work there? We thought, from the sounds and the strange smells from his furnace, that he must be at work on some form of alchemy, trying to change base metals into gold. Well, I have heard now what it really is, and I promise that it will surprise you!"

"Is it not alchemy, then?" asked Uncle Otto. "But we all know that he buys many kinds of metals, and that he mixes them and melts them over a furnace. And what of the young goldsmith that he hired only recently?"

"It is from that goldsmith, who is courting my granddaughter, that I heard the news," said old Peter. "He is making—printing—a book!"

"Printing a book!" Uncle Otto laid down his spoon in amazement. "You mean that he is making all that mystery about the printing of a book, a cheap, ugly block book such as are sold to poor people who can afford no better?"

"I know only what I heard. He told my granddaughter, and she told me, that Master Gutenberg is printing a book, a large book of many pages! And its so well done that no one could tell that it was not written by hand!"

Uncle Otto threw back his head and laughed. "Now I know that your young workman was but telling a tale to impress that granddaughter of yours! Well, we were all young once! *Printing* a book! Why, I myself have seen how they make those wooden blocks! The work is crude and ugly. The pictures are bad enough—but the script! No one could compare it with the work of a skillful scribe!"

"Well..." Old Peter looked disappointed. "Well, I only told you what she told me," he said.

"Gutenberg may indeed be printing there at his shop. That may be true," said Uncle Otto. "But mark my words! Unless he is also an alchemist, what would he want with all that metal? Yes, he is undoubtedly studying the methods of the ancient heathen sorcerers who were said to have changed lead and copper into gold, and that is why he is keeping his shop so closely guarded!"

Eagerly Karl listened. He had often passed the mysterious workshop on the outskirts of the city, had stared wonderingly at its barred windows and at the black smoke that poured from the chimney of the furnace. If the man were an alchemist, a sorcerer, why was it not possible that he had discovered some magic way of making books? What a wonderful thing *that* would be!

As Karl cleared the table and washed the bowls and spoons, a thought came to him. Tonight, when Uncle Otto was asleep, *he* would go to Gutenberg's workshop and try to find an entrance. *He* would learn the secret of this mystery!

As though they knew he was planning something, Uncle Otto and old Peter sat gossiping and talking in front of the fire on the hearth longer, it seemed, than ever before. At last Master Peter went to his own home, Uncle Otto to his curtained bed in the alcove, and Karl to his mattress of straw in the corner of the room.

When his uncle's regular snores at last announced that he was asleep, Karl unbarred the door, crept quietly out, and pulled it shut behind him. How dark it was outdoors! The overhanging houses almost met above his head and shut out all but a thin path of light from the moon as it rode high in the sky. Over the cobbles, through the twisting, dark streets Karl hurried until at last he came to the edge of the town. Here he could see the wide heavens and the bright, quiet moon shining down just as it did above the fields of his village home.

And there at last was the building that housed Master Gutenberg's establishment. Like most workshops, it was a two-story house with living quarters on the second floor for the owner and his workmen. Karl circled silently around the house and looked at each of the closed shutters in turn. He was beginning to think that his hopes were vain when he saw a place where the fastening had rusted away from the wall. Here was a chance!

Carefully, cautiously he moved the shutter. He was afraid that a creak of the rusty hinge might betray him. Though the house seemed dark and silent, some-one might be lying awake there. Now the shutter was open wide enough to admit a small, active body, and Karl mounted the sill. And there, with one leg in, and one out, he paused for a moment.

Looking down into the blackness inside, he felt a sudden shiver of fright that was not the fear of being discovered. He had remembered a picture he had once seen of a sorcerer—an alchemist! It was a picture of a cruel, hawk-nosed old man with a long beard, dressed in a flowing robe that was decorated with strange signs. The sorcerer was bent over a pot of some unearthly brew! Above his head bats and owls circled in the dark-ness. People said that alchemists and sorcerers worked with the Powers of Evil! Should he turn back? But his curiosity was far stronger than his fear; he slid off the sill and down into the workshop.

He noticed that it was not so dark as it had seemed at first. Enough of the moonlight came in through the barred openings close to the ceiling for Karl to see what was inside the room. Against the walls stood shelves filled with books. Heavy tables held what looked like piles of paper or vellum. In the middle of the room stood a tall, shadowy shape that drew his eyes at once. What could it be?

A framework, built of heavy timbers, reached from floor to ceiling. In the middle stood a massive table, and above this a huge screw hung from the top of the framework. It was as big around as a tree trunk! A projecting handle showed how it could be tightened or loosened. Karl saw with surprise that it was like the

178

cider presses he had often seen in the country! Was this, then, where they pressed out printings from the wooden blocks, just as Uncle Otto had said? There was no hint of magic here. Vaguely disappointed, Karl turned to the end of the room, where a red glow still lingered among the ashes of a small, low forge.

The tools, pans, and pots at the forge showed that they had been used for melting and mixing metals. But among them Karl saw no slightest trace of gold. He turned back again to the great press. Beside it stood a high, slanting desk, very much like the one Karl used. It was covered with a cloth. Karl was about to lift the cloth to see what was beneath, when something lying in a square of moonlight on the floor caught his eye. It was a tiny stick of metal. Karl picked it up and turned it over in his fingers. It was very small, but neatly and exactly made of lead or some similar heavy substance. One end was squared, and the other—Karl bent closer. He brought the stick more fully into the moonlight. On the other end a letter stood out in bold relief—the letter E, backwards!

For a long moment Karl stared down at this strange little object in complete bewilderment. Then an idea came to him. He pressed the carved end firmly against the flesh of his hand. For an instant the letter E showed plainly on his skin—the letter E, perfect and flawless and right side up! Then the impression on his hand began to fade.

His heart was beating thickly in his throat. He looked about on the floor for more of these lead sticks, but there were no others to be seen. Then he lifted the cloth that covered the desk. The slanting top was divided into many little boxes. All of them held hundreds of these same sticks of lead on each was carved a letter of the alphabet!

Then he saw something else. On a rack at the top of the desk was fastened a page. This finely written manuscript page was fastened as though ready for someone to copy it! But how, Karl wondered. Did they stamp the paper with each one of these little letters in turn? Then he saw the answer. A square frame held two columns of the stick letters, set together on end, and spaced into words to form a copy of the page! Instead of wooden blocks, the printing was done from this frame of letters!

Now Karl remembered the stacks of paper on the table. Examining them, the first ones he saw were blank. But at last he found what he was seeking. It was a sheet of fine paper—as fine as any that he had ever handled. And it was also the page of a book! A book, beautifully inscribed in letters that could not have been better written by Uncle Otto himself. Could *this* be printing? He picked up the next sheet, and the next. All were exactly alike without the slightest variation or difference. Magic? Sorcery? No, but fully as unbelievable, as marvelous as magic!

As he stood there with the page in his hand, Karl was suddenly torn from his dream. "What are you doing here, you thieving rogue?" cried a harsh voice. He looked up to see that a man with a cloak flung over his night clothing was standing over him with a thick, knotted staff grasped in his fist.

But for one more instant of time the wonder and surprise of his discovery still filled Karl's whole mind. "This page—why, it's *beautiful!*" he cried as he held up the sheet of paper. "This is as fine as the finest hand work!"

The man's scowl softened and he lowered his staff. "What's that? And who might you be, come at this hour to give me your praise?"

Then Karl recovered his senses enough to be thoroughly frightened at what he had done. Did the owner, Master Gutenberg, think him a thief? The penalties for stealing were harsh and cruel in the city of Strasbourg, Karl knew well! What was to become of him if he could not make the man understand that it was a desire to see this new work, not the wish to steal, that had brought him here! The only thing to do was tell his story. He squared his shoulders and began.

When he had finished, he stood looking fearfully up into the stern face. And then Master Gutenberg smiled. "I believe you, my lad. I will let you go free—but you must promise me never to do such a thing again. It is dangerous to prowl by night, and more so to come into other people's houses without leave! So you thought you found a secret spell by which books could be made to increase, did you?"

"Well, it seemed no more strange to me than to turn base metal into gold as others thought you were doing," Karl said sheepishly. "And it seemed to me that it would be a far better thing to do, if one had the power. It would be a noble magic indeed to make fine books—so many that even the poor could have them in place of the ugly block books."

"No, it is far removed from magic! It takes long, hard labor and much effort, although each week it seems we find ways to make it easier. Perhaps someday, God willing, it will be as you say, and books will be plentiful enough for the poor to own. What a world we shall have then! No, there is no magic nor mystery to it at all. But I have had many sad lessons that have taught me to guard my processes from those who would seize them and use them without leave. You see, it has taken me long years of my life and more gold than I dare to think of to work out my methods. I must earn enough by them now to pay back those who have trusted me."

Looking up at the tired, sad face, Karl suddenly felt a pity for this man. "Master Gutenberg! he said, laying a small, square hand on his arm, "I shall tell no one what I have seen here. I promise! And I *know* that you will soon earn back all that you have spent, because your work is so fine! My uncle is a scribe in the library of the Reverend Prior Paul and he has been teaching me the trade. So you understand that I know good work when I see it."

Gutenberg took the page that the boy held out to him. "Yes, it *is* good work," he said simply.

For a moment there was silence in the dim, moonlit room, for each was busy with his own thoughts. An idea had come to Karl—so bold an idea that he did not dare to stop to think it over before he put it into words. "Master Gutenberg! Do you have a place here for a boy—a boy who is strong and willing to work hard, and who wants more than anything in the world to learn your trade?" he asked.

Gutenberg looked down into the boy's face. Perhaps he was moved by Karl's frank and honest admiration, or perhaps it was the promise of loyalty that he saw there—loyalty of which he had seen so little. He spoke slowly. "Why, yes, I could take in another boy as apprentice," he said. "Now go home to your bed and I will go to mine. Come back in the morning and we will speak of this again."

He unbarred the door. Karl, too excited to do more than stammer his thanks, turned his face toward the sleeping city. But he would return! Yes, he would return again!

Q *ueen of the Sea*

WHEN TRADING AND COMMERCE increased in the latter part of the Middle Ages, the city of Venice in Italy became one of the richest and most powerful cities in the world. It was also one of the few cities that had a reliable and strong government. The city was ruled by a group of wealthy families, at the head of which was the Doge. All the business of the city was very strictly controlled and regulated. Many young Venetian men came to believe that because of this strict control there wasn't much chance for them to take part in new business ventures and to have personal success. Therefore they left Venice to go to other countries.

Trade with the East brought great riches to the Venetian merchants. But it wasn't always safe and easy. Caravans bearing goods from the Indies had to travel through lands that belonged to other countries. Many times these countries were unfriendly to Venetians. Often they charged the caravans heavy tolls, or taxes. The merchants knew that carrying goods by boat was much cheaper than carrying goods on land, but no one knew how to go by sea from Europe to the Indies. It was for these reasons that explorers began to look for a water route to the Far East.

Spain and Portugal took the lead in efforts to discover this new water route. The search went on for many years. Finally one route was discovered by a Portuguese navigator, Vasco da Gama. He sailed around the Cape of Good Hope, up the eastern side of Africa, through the Indian Ocean, across the Arabian Sea, to the city of Calicut on the western shore of India. His discovery gave Portugal the advantage in trade over Venice and other commercial cities. This advantage to Portugal, as you will read in the next story, was one of the reasons why Venice, once Queen of the Sea, began to decline in power and fame.

C AMILLA took a final, triumphant stitch and snapped off the thread. "There!" she said. "At last it is finished!" Jumping to her feet she shook out the bright scarlet velvet, with its patterns of gold braiding, for her mother to see. "I *know* Niccolo's father will be pleased with this!"

In the small, dark room that overlooked the green waters of a narrow side canal, the garment glowed like fire. Camilla's mother took it in her thin hands and looked it over carefully. "Yes, Master Jacopo can find no fault with this needlework," She smiled and patted her daughter's flushed cheek. "You have finished my task as well as I could have myself. Your skill with the needle may, indeed, be all that stands between us and hunger. If your brother Roberto does not return soon.... And yet thirteen years is too young to bear so heavy a burden!" She stopped as though suddenly very weary, and leaned back among the pillows of her couch.

Instantly Camilla was bending over her, anxiety in her blue eyes. "Do you feel ill again, mother? If you do, I shall stay here with you, and not go with Niccolo and his family when they call for me in the gondola!"

Her mother shook her head. "Not ill, only tired. And no medicine in the world would do me so much good as the thought that you are out in the sunshine with Master Jacopo's family, watching the procession and the great regatta.[1] You have been shut up in this dark room too long!"

For a moment more Camilla hesitated, then her face brightened again. "It *will* be wonderful, won't it? It seems so long since I have been to a festival. All of Venice will be there. They say that the floats of the different guilds and companies are more magnificent than were ever built before. The Doge himself will give out prizes to the finest!" Her eyes sparkled, and in her excitement she moved about the room on feet that seemed to dance. "And Niccolo told me that his father's crew, from the guild of the glass blowers, has a good chance to win the galley race! Oh, wouldn't it be glorious for me to see Master Jacopo, wearing this guild livery that I myself have made, steer the winning gal-

1. Boat races.

ley[1] to victory?"

A soft glow of pride shone in her mother's eyes as she watched the slender figure. Camilla was dressed in her best holiday gown, tight-bodiced, full-skirted, of soft blue wool, with snowy touches of linen at neck and wrists. A small, close-fitting cap of brightly embroidered blue velvet covered her head, and from under it Camilla's curls were a shower of red-gold, the color that the Venetian artists liked best of all to paint.

Suddenly in through the window came a peal of bells which were soon answered again and again by other bells. All the chimes in every tower of the city were ringing their welcome to the great Feast Day! With the sound of the bells came the whirr of doves' wings, as the startled birds filled the air. "Oh, hear the bells!" cried Camilla, running to the window. "It's almost time for the procession to start! *Why* doesn't Niccolo come?"

As if in answer, there was the sound of feet on the stairs and a knock at the door. Camilla ran to open it, and then drew back in dismay. "Why, what's the matter, Niccolo?" she cried.

Niccolo, son of Master Jacopo the glass blower, was two years younger than Camilla, but they were the best of friends. Now, as he stepped inside the single small room that was Camilla's home, she saw that his face was streaked and grimy, as though he had wiped away recent tears, and that he wore his ordinary clothing instead of his feast-day costume. "What is the matter?" she repeated, her heart beginning to pound.

1. A boat propelled by oars.

"Oh, Camilla!" began Niccolo. Then he stopped as though he hated to go on. "I've come for my father's costume. One of his customers from another city has arrived here in Venice, and they are taking *him* to the festival in our gondola! There won't be room for either of us, you or me!" He stopped, looked so unhappy that Camilla almost forgot her own disappointment in her pity for him. Swallowing with difficulty, Niccolo spoke again. "I brought the money for your mother's sewing, and my father wants me to hurry back."

Mechanically Camilla handed him the gleaming velvet. She heard the clink of the silver that he dropped into her palm, the quick slam of the door that closed behind him, and the sound of his feet on the stairs. But she saw nothing at all but the bright blur of her own tears. All at once the room seemed darker, chillier, damper, more dismal than ever before. With an abrupt gesture she flung the coins into a far corner, and turned to bury hear head in her mother's lap. What were silver coins to her when she must lose the pageantry, the gaiety, the beauty, that were more than bread to her young Venetian heart?

It would not have hurt her so much, she thought miserably, if things had always been like this! But until her father's death two years before, Camilla had lived a very different life. Luigi da Monote, her pleasant and easy-going father, had been born of a noble Venetian family. Instead of this one dark room on the sluggish backwater, they had lived in a small, pretty house. It had a sunny garden in the rear and a balcony that overhung a busy canal. From morning to night the gondolas, with their bright-colored tops, had glided upon its waters like tropic birds of brilliant plumage. How happy they had been there, and how suddenly all the happiness had vanished. For after Luigi died, his wife and daughter had found that he had left them nothing but debts.

Worst of all, during this past winter Camilla's mother had fallen ill of the fever, and seemed unable to win back her strength. How *could* she recover, thought Camilla wretchedly, when she had to sit sewing all day long in this damp, dark place? The only sunshine that ever came into the room was reflected in greenish ripples upon the ceiling from the canal below. The single charcoal burner that they could afford did not take away much of the room's chill. And, except for her mother, Camilla was quite alone.

Somewhere, it was true, she had an older brother, Roberto. But he had left his home long ago, and they had heard nothing of him for years. He had been a restless lad, eager to see what lay beyond the lagoons and tides of Venice. The Adriatic, even the great Mediterranean, had seemed too small for him. Like many another young Venetian, he had not been content to live under the close rules and restrictions of the all-powerful State of Venice. Such young men had found in other lands greater opportunities for their adventurous spirits. The last word that had come from Roberto was that he had shipped with a Portuguese captain, and had disappeared into the unknown seas along the coast of Africa.

Gradually, under her mother's gentle touch and

the soft, comforting murmur of her voice, Camilla's tears stopped. She began to feel a little ashamed of her childish outburst. After all, she was a great girl of thirteen, not a baby! She sat up and dried her eyes.

"Well, I suppose there will be other festivals. Maybe I'll see the next one." She tried to make her voice sound cheerful. "And these silver coins will bring in food for many a day to come. Look, Master Jacopo has sent more than he promised! He tried to make up for my disappointment. I *hope* his crew will win the race, even if I'm not there to see!"

As Camilla got to her feet and pushed the curls away from her hot face, a sound of rippling water and the creaking of an oar made her pause. "Listen! That sounds like a gondola! I thought all Venice would be out on the Grand Canal by this time. Do you suppose..." she said with sudden hope... "could they be coming for me after all?" Running to the window, she leaned over the rough stone of the sill.

A gondola was indeed moving upon the still, green water of their canal, but it was not Master Jacopo's. It was, however, stopping beside the tiny quay just outside their house, and the gondolier was speaking to someone hidden by the fringed canopy. Here you are, sir. Here is the house of the widow of Luigi da Monote. Up the stairs, the first door."

Camilla, almost falling out of the window in her curiosity, saw a man step from the boat to the flagstones of the quay. He was a broad-shouldered young man with a beard that glowed red in the sun. He looked up at the house. "*This* place! I think you must be mistaken, but I'll make sure. Wait here for me." He disappeared inside their lower doorway, his footsteps sounded on the stone of the stairs, and almost instantly Camilla heard a loud, firm knock on the door.

Wide-eyed, Camilla looked at her mother. "He reminded me of someone, but I don't know who!" she said.

Color flooded suddenly in her mother's thin cheeks. "Open the door!" she cried.

In the doorway the stranger blinked as though the dimness of their little room made it hard for him to see. "Pardon me for troubling you..." he began, "but I'm looking for..."

"Roberto!" Camilla heard her mother cry in a breathless voice. She struggled to her feet, scattering the pillows. In another instant she was caught in the arms of her son!

Then came tears and laughter and many explanations. Roberto's big voice and ruddy strength seemed to fill the little room with warmth and light, as he told them of his long voyage into uncharted seas. His bold captain, Vasco de Gama, had led his little fleet where no man had ever ventured before. They had sailed south to the very tip of Africa and then beyond, around it, northward again, following the coast, and finally crossed the stormy Indian Ocean to the rich city of Calicut itself! A new route had been opened to all the wealth of the Indies!

"Even my small share of our cargo of spices has brought me a fortune," he told them. "After our ships returned to Lisbon I took passage on the first vessel bound here for Venice, to see you all once more. I cannot stay long, for the King of Portugal is fitting out another fleet to make the voyage again, and has given me command of a vessel. But I shall not leave here until you are provided for, and safely settled back into your own house with the garden and the balcony. And why..." he continued, frowning suddenly, "why, when all of Venice is out upon the water, are you alone here in this dark little hole?

When Roberto heard their story, he startled them both by suddenly lifting his mother, pillows and coverlets and all, into his strong arms. "We'll go to the Festival! The procession has barely started." Laughing at his mother's protests, he strode down the stairs.

Camilla followed, feeling that it must all be a dream, a dazzling, wonderful dream. Then she remembered something. "Niccolo!" she cried. "Won't there be room for him too?"

On the steps before Master Jacopo's house, the mossy steps that led from the arched doorway down into the water, a small, dreary figure sat hunched, chin on hand. Camilla laughed aloud to see how round Niccolo's eyes grew as he recognized her in the gondola. But he needed no urging; he jumped in beside her, his face all one big smile.

Then out they glided into the moving pageant of color that was the Grand Canal. Roberto made the gondolier pause beside a flower-seller's barge while he bought wreaths and garlands of fresh country blossoms to deck themselves and their little vessel in honor of the holiday. They paused, too, at another barge for fruit and sweetmeats and delicious little cakes such as Camilla had not tasted in many a long day.

Just as they reached a point at which to stop, the Doge's barge, at the head of the great procession, appeared in sight. Proudly it swept along over the sunlit blue water. It was a splendid sight, with its guilding and painting, silken banners and pennants rippling in the wind. In the great cabin, as large as a hall of state, sat the Doge and all of the dignitaries of Venice. The three banks of oars were pulled by almost two hundred rowers in the richest livery. Musicians played sweet airs, but the sound barely carried across the canal because the cheers of the crowds in the boats along its path drowned out all but the loudest strains.

Close behind came a series of other rafts, floats, and barges. These had been built by the various guilds and merchant companies. All were gay with color and gorgeous or fantastic in design. Suddenly a raft drew near the appearance of which brought a hush of surprise and wonder across the crowded water. On the raft a furnace had been built in the shape of a great sea monster from whose mouth and nostrils shot flames.

"It's the barge of the glass blowers of Murano!" cried Niccolo, standing up in his excitement. "My father told me what it was going to be like!"

As they rode upon the raft, the skilled workmen of the guild dipped their long, hollow blow pipes into the melted glass, and then and there, before the eyes of the crowd, blew the finest of crystal goblets to be used, so the rumor went, in the Great Palace banquet-hall that very night!

Then came more barges, so many that Camilla's eyes were dazzled and Niccolo's throat grew hoarse with cheering. At last Roberto told their gondolier to make his way farther out into the lagoon, nearer to the long flat stretch of the Lido.[1] "We must find a good place to watch the galley races," he said.

Camilla and Niccolo were glad that they rode with so skillful an oarsman! Somehow, by edging between boats through spaces that seemed impossibly narrow, and by rowing so hard that his genial brown face dripped with sweat, the gondolier managed to bring them to a place exactly on the finish line. "We'll see perfectly from here!" cried Niccolo, gleefully. He climbed out into the narrow bow of the gondola, and seated himself astride the high, beaked prow.

A moment later, another gondola, large and richly gilded, and propelled by two men in handsome liveries, pulled into the space beside them. Under the fringed and tasseled silken canopy sat a group of ladies and gentlemen so grandly dressed that Camilla felt sure they must live in the most magnificent of the palaces that lined the Grand Canal itself. A man in purple velvet, the youngest of the company, looked intently at Roberto as their boats drew alongside one another, and lowered the lute upon which he had been playing.

"Are you not Roberto da Monote?" he asked.

"Yes, Messer, that is my name," answered Camilla's brother.

"I saw you at the Custom House this morning as

1. A strip of land which formed the shore of the lagoon on which the boats were to race.

you were getting off a ship that had just docked from Lisbon. There is a wild rumor flying about the Rialto[1] that Portuguese vessels have rounded the tip of Africa and actually reached the Indies by that route. Do you know if there is truth in that rumor, Master Monote?"

The other gentlemen in the boat were listening now, their faces sharply alert. "Yes, it is true," answered Roberto calmly. "I know, because I myself was aboard the ship of Master Vasco da Gama. We did indeed reach Calicut, and returned with a great cargo of spices, and also with a treaty signed by the ruler of the city himself."

The young man struck his hand upon the side of the boat. "Did I not tell you?" he cried as he turned to the others. "Why must you wise men of Venice never see that the world is changing? The Turks have blocked our trade in the Eastern Mediterranean. If we had allowed our captains to follow their own desires, and seek new routes, as did the Portuguese, *we* might have made that treaty ourselves. This is blindness! Our trade in spices is the very basis of our commerce!"

But the older men, after a short moment of alarm, smiled and shook their heads. "The State must decide these things," said one. "We can make treaties with the Turks," said another. "Such a long voyage—too hazardous for profit!" said a third. And the fourth, a thin-lipped man, smiled sourly. "I remember that you said we had missed a great chance when that Genoese —what was the fellow's name—Christopher Columbus,

1. A bridge across the Grand Canal which became a famous place of trade.

made a long voyage into the West for Spain a few years ago. And we all know nothing of value has come of *that*!" he added scornfully. "Venice is as always, Queen of the Sea!"

Before the young man could reply, a high, clear trumpet call and a shout from the crowd announced that the race was about to begin. Camilla stood up and steadied herself against her brother's broad shoulder. Even her mother, she saw happily, was sitting eagerly erect with color in her cheeks and a new brightness in her eyes.

The crowd grew silent as it waited for the final starting signal. Across the bright water Camilla could see the row of galleys, small in the distance like gulls resting on the surface. "I think the glass blowers are second from the left," said Niccolo, squinting his eyes against the light. "Farthest to the left are the leather workers. They won the race last year, and so they are the favorites. But I know that we shall win this time, because my father is steering for us!"

Then the trumpet pealed again; the oars dipped down, flashed up, and the galleys swept forward upon the water. Instantly the silence was shaken by a deafening roar of cheers. Every single person in the mass of boats that covered the lagoon like a many-hued carpet was cheering for one or another of the racing crews! Camilla cheered too; her voice sounded shrill above the din.

On and on the galleys came, their oars lifting and falling with swift precision. Soon it was plain that of them all the two boats farthest to the left were outdistancing the rest. They grew larger and larger as they neared the finish. Camilla could not tell which was leading, but Niccolo had no doubts! "The glass blowers are ahead! See, Camilla, there's my father's red doublet! They're ahead!" He stood up, balanced on the narrow prow.

Suddenly there was a grown from the crowd. In the glass blowers' galley someone had broken an oar! The steady rhythm was broken, only for a second, but long enough to lose the slight lead they held. Now the figureheads on the two boats were side by side and the crowd grew frantic. Then slowly, inch by inch, Master Jacopo in his scarlet tunic moved ahead of the other steersman. The glass blowers' galley crossed the finish line first, while the sky itself rang with cheers; roses and garlands, tossed from boat to boat, filled the air!

"They've won! Oh, Niccolo!" cried Camilla, with wild joy. And then "Niccolo!" she repeated in terror. For Niccolo was nowhere to be seen!

There was a splash and a splutter beside her. Looking down, Camilla saw a dark head bob up in the water. "I got so excited I fell in," explained Niccolo, as though Camilla could not see that for herself! "But I saw them win! I saw my father win!"

Roberto reached down and plucked Niccolo out of the water, none the worse for his dunking. The race was won! The glass blowers' galley drew up beside that of the Doge, and they could see Master Jacopo's red tunic plainly as he climbed up to receive the prize from the hand of the Doge himself. And again the crowd cheered and tossed flowers, and every bell tower in

Venice pealed its chimes in answer!

Then back over the water glided their gondola. It carried, small though it was, as large a load of happiness as any in all Venice. The sun had begun to set; under a sky of flame and rose they moved upon the water that reflected the colors of the sky like a vast fire-opal. The level rays touched the dome of Saint Mark's and the Lion,[1] and burnished the already golden palaces of the merchant princes, those merchants who, through their trade with the Orient, had built this city to be the marvel of all the world.

In some of those palaces there were many who lay awake far into that night. Wiser than the rest of the merchants, they knew well that another sun on that day had set over Venice! The news that Roberto's ship had brought from Portugal meant that the reign of the Queen of the Sea was at long last drawing to its end. Venice was losing its power and fame throughout the world.

But Camilla and her mother slept peacefully, while the moonlight turned the canals to silver, and, in the garden of the little house that would soon be theirs again, a nightingale sang all night long.

1. Saint Mark's is a large cathedral. The Lion is a bronze lion mounted on a tall column near the Doge's palace.